A Glimpse into

Madness

SeanWalter.Author@Gmail.com

Ordering information: Discounts may apply for bulk quantities for businesses and other commercial applications. For details, contact the author at the web address listed above, or the distributor at www.IngramContent.com

ISBN: 978-0-9960947-0-2

Printed in the United States of America

Dedicated to Pink and Leah, my very first fans and to everyone who ever gave me a free coffee.

About the author:

I have started this several times without much gain. I mean, honestly, how does one talk about themselves for any length of time without actually knowing who will be reading it? It's mind-boggling. Do you start it off like you would an AA meeting? "Hello, my name is Sean Walter, and I'm a writer"? It confuses me.

Which is why I decided to skip the whole intro thing, and move right along to telling you something about myself. I'm twenty-eight years old. I was born and raised in Portland, Oregon – which is not the Portland, Oregon that one can see in television shows or online entertainment. My Portland is a night-city. Its streets are empty, save for the homeless, the drugged, or the stumbling drunk. It's peaceful for the most part, but it can be dangerous. If you are young, attractive, and alone, I would not travel through certain sections of my night-city.

I've worked many jobs in my life. I've been a bouncer, a butcher, a janitor, protection for a call girl. I've spent time as a clerk, a phone specialist, a crate-maker and packer, as security for orgies, and as an EMT. I've met interesting people, and I've despised some of them, and loved some of them, and even both at once. I've yet to travel more than a thousand miles from home, but it's a start.

People fascinate me. I study them. I'll study you, if you spend much time with me. I'll learn your mind, your reactions, your lies, your hidden secrets, and I'll keep them for myself.

I'm greedy in that way.

If you'd like to contact me directly, please feel free to email me: SeanWalter.Author@Gmail.com. I'd love to hear from you.

About the book:

The book which you hold is full of stories that I've dwelt upon for more time than I care to admit. They are mostly fictitious. There are some true stories mixed in here and there, but you will have to find those for yourself. It's much more fun that way. I honestly wonder if you can find them all.

Over the last few years I've written, and thought, and rewritten, and grown, and edited, and desired, and complained, and written, and drank copious amounts of coffee, and thought some more, and written, and written, and written, and emerged with a book. It's a fun and scary thing to delve into your own mind and poke things with a stick, to awaken them, to make them real with ink and paper. They stare back at you, then, seeing themselves in your eyes, blinking in the synthetic lights of an all-night diner.

These stories *are* alive, mind you. They will read you as you read them, and they will be confused, and startled, and they may even fall in love. I hope they will. I hope they find your touch soothing. I hope they think your eyes are akin to endless forests full of wonder and mystery. I hope they find a comfortable place in your mind in which to watch your life unfold.

This is a simple glimpse into my world. I will allow you to play with my friends and to dance with my demons for a time, just remember the old advice from Nietzsche: "When you gaze long into an abyss the abyss also gazes into you."

Welcome to my world.

Table of Contents

The Night the Dolls Came

The chill winter wind blew from the east, trying with all its might to blow away the small town full of tiny, twinkling lights that lay in its path. It shook the windows in their frames in Susie's bedroom. Her young mind conjured up a collection of monsters that were trying, desperately, to break in and gobble her up, then they would go for her sisters. Her parents would awaken the next morning and lament not installing better windows. Another violent gust hit the house, sending tremors through her treasured porcelain doll collection on its high perch.

Susie squirmed lower under her blankets and shivered. She watched the shadows dance on the walls and listened to the howls of ghosts long dead coming out of the chimney. Her eldest sister had told her all about them last Halloween – how the house was constructed on an old cemetery, and how, try as they might, they could never locate thirteen of the bodies. Her mother said the sound was just the wind, but she knew better. After all, her sister wouldn't lie, and parents were always making up lies so as not to scare her.

She steeled her nerves and got out of bed. Her bladder would not allow her to remain idle any longer, and she dared not wet the bed again. It had been months since the last time, and she took it as a point of pride when she awoke in the morning to dry sheets.

She got to the bathroom down the hall and used the toilet. The seat was cold, which she hated, but she knew that if she took too long, a vengeful spirit would emerge from one of the mirrors to drag her off, and her family would never see her again. She finished as quickly as she could and avoided looking at any of the mirrors as she washed her hands in the moonlight. She caught a glimpse of one mirror, on accident, as she was leaving, and could have swore that an old crone was glaring out at her through stitched-shut eyes, with her bony arms resting on her decaying hips.

Susie ran down the hallway and dove into her bed. She burrowed her way from the bottom of her blankets to her pillow, then crawled around in a circle three times, just as her dog did, to get comfortable. It never seemed to work for her. She was just beginning to wonder why her dog did it at all when one of her porcelain dolls fell from its high perch and landed with a crack on the wood floor. Susie started, and stared at the fallen doll, watching for any movement. The shadows on the walls continued to dance, and the windows still shook in their frames, but nothing else stirred.

Slowly, she leaned herself towards the foot of her bed, then crawled to the edge. She stared at the doll intently, not even blinking, like a cat unsure if what it saw was predator or prey.

Then the doll slowly lifted its cracked head and looked at her, its dead eyes staring as only dolls can. Susie tried to scream, but fear had stolen her voice. Instead, she turned and threw her blankets over her head, certain that they would protect her. She tried not to breathe as she listened to the doll's tiny footsteps run back and forth in the room.

"Su-u-u-sie," a small, sweet voice called out from the darkness, "where did you go?"

Chills ran down Susie's spine. "Go away," she said, trying to keep her voice steady. She felt a tug on her blanket and immediately regretted saying anything. The doll was on the bed with her, walking above the covers, getting closer with every passing second.

"Su-u-u-u-sie," the doll called to her. She felt the weight of it on her leg, making small steps up to her stomach. "Su-u-u-u-u-sie."

In a flash, Susie flung the doll off of her, throwing her blanket to the foot of her bed with the effort. She

3

reached down and pulled the blanket back over her head as quickly as she could, only then realizing that she never heard the doll land.

She listened for any movement in the room, eyes shut tight, but even after several minutes, she heard nothing. *What if it's hanging from the ceiling?* She thought of the old brass chandelier that hung in her room, and imagined the doll there – pictured it staring at her bed with its porcelain smile, frozen forever in forced pleasantry. Would it wait for her?

Slowly, carefully, she pulled the blanket from her face. She opened her eyes, and gasped. Before her lay a sea of pale dolls. Every flat surface of her room was covered in them, and all of them were looking at her, sitting, waiting in menacing silence. She wanted to run, but where could she go? The doll with the cracked head sat on her bed, at her feet. It laughed, cheerfully, and said, "Susie! There you are! Let's play!"

And then the moon went out.

There was a rustling in the darkness. The air moved around Susie as she sat, unable to budge. Even in the midst of absolute terror, she felt a solemn guilt when she noticed that she had wet the bed, despite her earlier journey. Tears fell hotly down her face, more out of shame than out of fear.

And then the moon lit up, and the dolls were gone. Along with her shelf, and her toy chest, and her bed.

At first she was elated that she had not, in fact, wet the bed but had wet the floor, instead. Then she began to wonder where exactly all of her belongings had gone. She looked around her bare room until her eyes fell upon a standing shadow. It was smiling at her through darker lips and a single smokey grey eye. She wished she still had covers to hide under.

"Don't be scared," said the shadow in the voice of a small boy, no older than she was, "I chased them away. I couldn't stop them from taking your things, though." His voice was full of sympathy and remorse.

"Thank you," Susie replied, quietly, and meant it. "What's your name?" she asked.

"Jacob," replied the shadow. The windows rustled and shuddered in their frames. "A horrible night, isn't it?"

Susie nodded. "What happened to the moon just now?"

Jacob shuffled his shadowed feet and looked at, presumably, the floor. "That was me. I had to distract them. I'm sorry if it scared you."

As far as Susie was concerned, if he was sorry, everything was alright. "What are you?" she asked, unable to resist the question any longer.

"Just a shadow," Jacob said, and chuckled, "What else could I be?"

"You could be a demon," Susie replied, sure of herself.

"You've met the closest thing to a demon in these parts. Besides, demons are...pointier."

Susie conceded with a nod. "But where did you come from?"

5

"Oh, I've always been here. I have to be, there's nowhere else to go."

Susie looked at him, curiously. "Are you real?" she asked, innocently.

"Of course I'm real. Are you?"

She glared at him. "It's not polite to ask someone if they're real or not," she said, as haughtily as she could manage.

"But you asked me first," the shadow pleaded.

"That's different. You're in my room." Susie was sure this was the proper way of doing things. Almost as an afterthought, she continued, "And besides, you're a boy. It's okay to ask boys that kind of thing."

"Gosh, I didn't know that. I'm sorry."

Susie nodded, curtly, certain that some unspoken protocol had been observed. "Can I hug you?" she asked. Jacob seemed to demure. His head fell low, and he started to fidget.

"I don't think you can," he said, finally. "I'm not all here, you see." He shuffled on the wall just above the floor, then lifted his head with a jolt, and said excitedly, "But if you really want to do something for me, you can... that is, if you want to, you can..." he faltered.

"What?" Susie asked.

"...You could give me a kiss," the shadow said, finally.

"Is that all?" Susie laughed, then stood up and walked to the wall that Jacob was splayed against. She stood up on tip-toe to reach, and kissed him on what she assumed to be his cheek. Jacob smiled, broadly.

"Thank you," he said. His tone grew suddenly lower, "Uh-oh, I've got to go. It'll be dawn soon, and the sun will chase me away."

"Don't be silly. Everyone knows that the dawn only scares away bad things, and you're not evil, Jacob."

The shadow hung his head once more. "You don't know that," he replied.

"Well, you can't go," Susie said, "I forbid it."

"I have to. You don't understand... I can't see the sunlight. Never again." Susie could hear the tears that Jacob was shedding, even though she couldn't see them. "I'm dead, Susie."

A chill crept across Susie's body as he spoke those words, and the cold pit in her stomach told her that what he said was true, but she refused to believe any of it. Then she, too, began to cry. "Will you come back?" she asked.

"I can't, not for a long time. I could only come tonight to save you. It's just the way things work."

Jacob began to fade as the sky outside Susie's window grew lighter. She reached out and tried to hold his hand, but all she felt was the cold wall, and when she pulled back, only her own shadow remained. "Goodbye," she heard Jacob say from somewhere perhaps far away, but it could have been the wind.

Susie went to the center of her room and sat down. "Don't go," she whispered, sadly, and whatever beings there were who answered the pleas of small children ignored her. She went right on crying straight through the morning's twilight.

7

The sun peeked over the distant hills to find her slumped in the middle of her empty bedroom floor. She blinked at the rising dawn through red eyes and faded complexion and wondered what kind of life it was that would allow the sun to rise after such a night.

She rose and opened her bedroom door, automatically heading for her parents' bedroom. On her way she passed the bathroom, and once again she saw the old crone in the mirror. She stopped and went inside, still afraid, but no longer caring. The crone twitched her sewn eyes at her like a short eclipse of cold stone in a cloudy sea from the world behind the glass. "What's wrong, girl?" the crone asked, bluntly.

"Jacob went away, and the dolls took my bedroom, and I don't know what to do," Susie let out a sob that shook her small body.

"All that?" the crone tsk'd. "Stop crying, girl. Crying will get you nowhere at all." Susie did her best to stop the flow of tears. "Good," the crone continued, "Now, it's a shame about Jacob, he was a nice boy, but then he's not really gone, is he?"

Susie shrugged. "I don't know. I guess not. I mean, he said he was always here."

"You see?" The crone smiled, and it was not an evil smile. "As for your bedroom, you just have to tell the dolls that it's yours, and you want it back."

Susie blanched. "But they're so scary! They'll take me away, I know they will!"

The crone let out a laugh that sounded like sandpaper rhythmically rubbing against wood, and her

8

brittle frame shook. "If they try to take you away, just tell them Mary has claimed you already."

"But... does that mean you're going to take me, instead?" Susie asked, meekly.

"Oh yes, in time."

Susie hung her head in defeat. Quietly, she began to sob.

"But not today." The crone said, slyly, then winked at her, and faded away, leaving Susie staring in awe at her own reflection.

Susie stood in the hallway for a long time, deciding what to do. She marched back to her bedroom with more confidence than she felt. The dolls were waiting for her there, impervious to the morning light that shown through her window. As a group, all of them turned their heads to her, with the cracked-headed doll in front. "Su-u-u-u-sie," it called in its sweet voice.

"I'd like my room back, please," Susie said.

The dolls all giggled in unison. "We like it. We're going to keep it." The cracked doll stood up. "We like you, too, Susie."

"You can't have me, and you can't have my room," Susie said, indignant.

"Why?" the cracked doll giggled.

"Because Mary claimed me already."

The dolls looked around at each other, their beaded eyes questioning the matter, weighing what might come of it. Then, one by one, they all began to vanish in whiffs of white smoke. After a few moments, only the cracked doll remained. It looked up at Susie, and said, sadly, "We just wanted to play," then fell limp to the ground.

As it hit the floor, Susie's furniture all appeared back in its rightful place, as if it had never left at all. Susie smiled and crawled into bed. As exhaustion took her, she wondered if, one day, she would be taken by the old crone in the mirror, and what kind of world it was that she lived in, but, she decided, that was for another day, and peacefully fell asleep.

Writer's Block

I have nothing to write. Nothing at all.

No long winded speeches on the fallacy of moral codes, or the limits of group thinking.

No great descriptions of the color of flame, the smell of a winter's day in the city, the look in a beautiful woman's eyes.

I have no reason to write about the downfall of one man's simple life, his concealment of numerous affairs, his debts to the mob, his suicide.

I cannot mention the people who live in the walls, who visit me in my dreams. Nor can I tell you of how much they miss me when I don't see them.

I think I could write about rodents, but they won't let me interview them. They just scurry away, back into the fields or the cracks in the pavement, and flick their little pink noses at me, in scorn, from the darkness.

Would that I could write of grand battles between hoards of dried leaves, their brittle stems a self-defeating combination of sword and brainstem, and a lesson in duality to a curious observer.

I may write about the devil, the lord of the flies, the most-unclean, the fallen angel, god's favorite. I wonder what he thinks when he's alone at night, and if he likes his role. If he would take it all back, or, perhaps, take it further.

But no. I have nothing to write. Not tonight. No ideas flow through the ether into my impatient mind. The muse laughs at my feeble attempts at coherent thought, her cackles echoing into the shadow of dawn.

I have nothing to write.

The Windup

Click...
Click...
Click...

Mary was born to a simple family in a suburban town. Her mother, a bit of an eccentric woman, collected artwork from painters who were in ill health, and then waited for them to die so she could resell them at a profit. Her father worked behind a desk shuffling papers and cataloguing. Mary received an education at a public school, which left her fairly well rounded, she assumed, and gave her a subtle distaste for people who went to private schools.

After graduating high school with a moderate grade average, she took a year off in which to "find herself" by drinking, fucking, and getting into trouble on a regular basis. A year later she started attending a local college which had a handful of very gifted professors, but overall, she felt, it was shit. But it was in this school that the two most profound things in her life took place.

The first happened when she was in a psychology course with one of the more gifted professors. The professor, on a tangent, went into great detail about the origins of life, lending great credence to both the scientific and the spiritual approaches, but then went on to explain the abstract. "What if," he was often quoted as saying, "life began because somebody, somewhere in the future, stepped on the peel of a Squigglesnort?" a Squigglesnort being a wholly alien fruit remarkably resembling a banana, with the key difference of having a peel with a variable mass which attracts passing feet to step on it to begin life and create universes. Mary filed that whole ordeal under "ludicrous" and only once ever thought about it again.

The second most profound thing in Mary's life happened a few months later, when a boy asked her out on a date, which she accepted due to reasons of hunger. The boy was an absolute bore and a cretin, but while on the date she snuck away and obtained the number of a gorgeous woman who was their waitress and who had listened with great interest to Mary's short retelling of a television show involving robots that hardly anyone saw while the boy sat looking on in wonder, playing with his fork.

Mary and the waitress, who's name was Francesca, became romantically involved after a sufficiently prolonged game of *Are You Attracted to the Same Sex, Too?* The process was filled with countless missteps, several awkward moments, and one or two near misses that almost resulted in them never speaking to one another again. It all culminated in a romantic bout of passion in front of a bewildered group of friends who weren't in on the game and never thought to ask.

Francesca eventually quit her job as a waitress to get another as a secretary under the title of Personal Assistant – a title that often made her chuckle because she had the sort of mind that related anything to sex. Mary worked various jobs in and around the city in which they lived, some better than others, but more or less managed to get by. The two eventually married, and made several attempts to make Mary pregnant via artificial insemination, none of which succeeded and all of which caused a great deal of emotional damage to the both of them. Eventually they decided to adopt a small boy whose parents had simply been too young to take care of him.

The child, Jake, was a handful. During his childhood, he constantly got into fights and worried his parents with his various injuries. Francesca and Mary had a fair share of arguments and rough patches, both struggling, as the years went by, with the idea that life wasn't at all like they thought it would be when they were children. Those were dreams that neither had ever truly given up.

Around the time Jake was in his late teens, Francesca was diagnosed with several forms of verocious cancers, and began to undergo a radical series of treatments which were only mildly effective. On the day she died, Francesca was sitting in bed, propped up by pillows as she no longer had the strength for much else, and was repeatedly winding a music box she had inherited from her grandmother.

Mary sat in a nearby chair, sometimes keeping up conversation, sometimes simply being there in the company of the woman she loved, watching her windup the music box and listening to the hollow, grating, metallic tones that somehow soothed her troubled mind. She eventually dozed off, and was only awoken by a deafening silence.

She spent the next several years recovering from the loss of her wife. When Jake became engaged, it stirred something in her that she didn't care to remember, and caused her to reject his fiancée utterly. The strong willed man that she had taught him to be rejected her in return, and they became estranged for nearly a decade over it. Mary spent that decade merely existing: sometimes becoming involved with other people, but never seriously. Sometimes becoming a user of various drugs, but never seriously.

In the end, it was Jake's wife, Melissa, who brought them back together and helped mend two ruptured souls. The remainder of Mary's years were spent spoiling her two grandchildren and pursuing different and interesting fancies. She spent her last days in a hospital bed, visited often by her son and his wife and children, and that gave her some joy. But what most made her happy was the music box she kept on her lap – the same that Francesca had played on her deathbed. She would wind it up, sometimes, and watch the turnkey spin as the notes came to life, and suddenly she was reminded of a day back in college, when a silly professor went into the abstract ideas behind the origins of life. She recalled what he had said about the Squigglesnort and smiled to herself.

"To step on a piece of fruit and start life itself," she thought, "that's just silly." She wound the music box once more, and listened to the tune play out in its own time. "Well... maybe not *too* silly."

She wound the music box for the last time, and chuckled in a halfhearted, hopeful way.

Click...
Click...
Click...

Etiquette

Amanda sat in the near-freezing puddle of mud behind her house, making polite little mud-men out of dirt, and sticks, and tea. Her discarded teacup lay cracked on the lawn a little ways off. She went into great detail with the earl grey scented creatures, even going so far as to make little wigs for them. She was just about to fashion a little pet mud-dog when her mother came around the corner of the house and spotted her.

"Amanda!" she shrieked, "Get away from there this instant!" She marched forward and pulled the young girl from the ground. "Look at you. You've ruined your dress," she said as she led Amanda toward the house. "Get inside and have Emilie give you a bath. We will be attending church soon, and a proper young lady should be clean."

She left the girl standing in the doorway, wondering if her mud-men would be alright without their dog to protect them from the worms and passing cats. Emilie walked down the stairs smiling and shaking her head. "Miss Amanda, what have I told you? You cannot play in the mud unless your mother will be out for a good long time."

"I know, Emilie," Amanda said, sweetly, looking at the floor. "I just wanted to do it for a little while."

"Well, come on then. Let's get you cleaned up."

The bath went well. Emilie had set out a new blue summer dress in the dressing area for her. The frills were of a darker lace, and it came with one of her favorite things – a black ribbon choker. There was a thick matching shawl next to it, but, trying it on in the mirror, she couldn't see the choker anymore, so she left the shawl behind. She grabbed her favorite doll as a vaccine against boredom during church and for company.

After dressing, her mother came and collected her. Their carriage pulled around the long driveway and up to the main entrance, they boarded and were off. Margarette, Amanda's mother, glared at the doll Amanda kept clutched to her chest. "You're getting too old for dolls, dear," she chided. Amanda held the doll tighter.

The carriage dropped them at the churchyard gates and they walked through the chill autumn air to the grand entrance. Before the doors stood the Vicar, greeting people by name as they entered. Margarette stopped and smiled pleasantly. "Good day," she said. "You remember my daughter Amanda?"

"Of course," he replied, jovially. "How are you today, Miss Amanda?"

Amanda shrugged in reply. She tugged at her mother's dress. "I'm cold, Mama," she said.

"That's 'mother,' dear," she replied, then turned back to the Vicar.

"But I'm *cold*," Amanda pleaded.

"Amanda, be quiet. It's rude to interrupt."

She held her doll across her chest. Her mother carried on the conversation with the Vicar, but Amanda ignored it. Time seemed to drag forward for her, reluctantly giving up every second like a drowning man gives up air. She wished she could go back to the warm water she had bathed in, or at least that she had brought her thick shawl.

At last, the Vicar told them to take their seats, and that mass was about to start. They went inside and sat down near the front on the cold wooden pews. Amanda shifted uncomfortably in her seat, trying to move closer to her mother.

"Stop fidgeting," her mother told her, and shot a glare at her to let her know she meant it.

The Vicar preached a sermon all about honoring thy father and thy mother, and shared a conspiratorial smile with Margarette. A repetitive clicking periodically resounded throughout the front rows. Several parishioners began looking around for the source of the noise until Margarette took Amanda by the hand and lead her, and her chattering teeth, outside.

At home, Margarette sent her daughter straight to bed, taking her doll away and refusing even to let Emilie in to start the fire or replace the heating stones in her bed. Amanda shivered all night long, drawing her legs against her chest beneath the covers to keep the draft out.

She greeted the next morning with a chest-shattering cough. When her father tried to call the family doctor, Margarette argued with him. "She's faking it, just trying to make me look horrible," she said, but made sure Emilie went into the room every half hour to fuel and stoke the fire, relieving her of any further duties for that day.

"I'm bored, Emilie," Amanda whined upon waking in the late afternoon.

"You're sick, miss. You need your rest."

Amanda, in the way of children everywhere, knew that if she were not sick, she would be able to get out of bed, and thus no longer be bored, and so instantly decided that she felt better and attempted to spring from her bed. She got as far as throwing off her heavy top blanket and quilt before giving up. She plopped back onto her feather pillows, out of breath and shivering. "Could you bring me my doll?" she asked as sweetly as she could manage. Emilie smiled and nodded, then walked out of the bedroom.

She snuck down to the parlor silently, as only servants taught not to be heard can. Margarette sat at the piano, seemingly reading the music she held in her hand. How she managed to do that while staring out of the large window into the garden is anyone's guess.

Emilie retrieved the doll from Margarette's hiding place behind an armoire, and left the room like a ghost blowing under the parlor doors. Amanda was fast asleep, but Emilie tucked the doll under her arm and pulled the heavy blankets up to her chin. She stayed a few moments in silence, listening to Amanda breathe. She could have sworn she was listening to the gardener rake the gravel paths in the first spring thaw, when the stones are still half frozen to one another. She added more fuel to the fire and changed the heating stones in the mattress under Amanda's feet before quietly leaving and shutting the doors behind her.

Margarette was waiting in the hallway. "How is the little liar?" she spat.

"She's having trouble breathing, Ma'am. I don't think she's pretending," Emilie finished, quietly.

"*You*? *You* think? Who in the world cares what a serving girl thinks?!" Margarette shouted.

"Yes ma'am, sorry ma'am," Emilie stammered, bowing herself away down the hall.

Margarette waited until she was out of sight, then opened the bedroom door as quickly as she could and peered in. She expected to catch Amanda out of bed, playing about the room, but to her surprise, her daughter lay completely still, asleep, in bed. The heat of her fury was instantly quenched in a pool of worry. She crossed the room and stood near the bed, holding her hands together near her waist, as her mother had always insisted. She moved her eyes to look over her daughter's pale countenance, leaving her head stationary.

Amanda's chest rose and fell beneath the covers, barely moving them. Margarette looked over her shoulder at the open bedroom door, then back to Amanda. She crossed the room, closed the door, locked it, and returned. She took one more look back at the door, then, finally, bent down and felt Amanda's forehead with the back of her hand. She moved it to her cheek and back again, then shook her head sadly, and brushed Amanda's hair out of her sleeping face.

The child rolled toward her touch, pulling the covers down to her elbow, exposing the doll she cradled. Margarette blinked at it, wondering how it had gotten there, then she glared. She tore the doll from Amanda's loving embrace. The girl awoke as her mother crossed the room with the doll. "Mama, no!" she cried, but it was too late. The doll wilted and burned upon the fire.

Days passed, and Amanda's illness worsened. She refused to see her mother, going so far as to throw a bedpan at her when she came near. Finally, Margarette broke down and sent Emilie to fetch the doctor. As Emilie left, Margarette marched into Amanda's room.

"Dear," she started, with a voice like molasses, "the doctor is coming. He's going to make you feel better."

The girl rolled away from her.

"Amanda, we must make you presentable," her mother continued, looking at the sweat-soaked sheets and bile-stained blankets. "Let's get you in the tub and cleaned up before he arrives. We must not embarrass ourselves."

"Go away," Amanda grumbled, then fell to coughing.

"Amanda, you can't receive visitors in this state. It's shameful!" The girl didn't stir. A thought occurred to Margarette. "What if I get you a new doll? Would you like that?"

The pale girl turned towards her mother. "Can she have a red dress like mine?" she asked, hopefully.

"Of course, dear, whatever you want."

She thought about it for a moment, then reached her arms out to her mother.

"Oh!" Margarette gasped, backing away from her daughter's stained nightgown. "No, dear. Let me call Geoffrey. He'll get you out of bed."

As the doctor walked into Amanda's sick-ward, he saw the perfect little girl, propped up against her headboard on new, crisp sheets, covered in the finest night clothes, her hair in loose curls. She even had rouge on her lips and cheeks, providing color where there was none. Margarette stood nearby, hands clasped in front of her waist, back straight, beaming. "Good day, doctor," she said.

Spring arrived with all the warmth and joy that winter had stolen from the house. Amanda lay in a brand new dress, her hair done up in the latest style, her face made up, her hands in a place of comfort, folded over her stomach. Margarette noticed a slight blue/black bruise on the back of Amanda's forearm. Burns, the mortician had said, from keeping her body on ice until the thaw came and they could dig a proper grave. She directed one of his helpers to apply more makeup to the area in a cold tone.

The service was moving, the Vicar having had plenty of practice during such a long and cold winter. After its conclusion, before they closed the casket, Margarette pulled something from the folds of her petticoats, and placed it under Amanda's cold arm. She could have sworn the child's lifeless body cuddled it.

Emilie had made up her mind – she could no longer work for such a monstrous woman. She didn't even care if she received a reference, anything was better than staying here. She marched into the mistress's bedchamber with more dignity than she'd felt in years. "Madam?" she called, opening the door.

There was no answer.

She looked around for some clue as to the whereabouts of her soon to be ex-employer, and saw the door leading to the powder room ajar. She walked in on tiptoe, and there she found Margarette.

She lay in her nicest bathing-gown in a full tub. Her hair was done up with ribbons, her face as calm as a statue, her wrists splayed open, resting at her sides, dying the water a deep crimson. The blue pallor of death was just beginning to come over her.

And somewhere in the darkness of the earth, below the unfeeling and unforgiving soil, sat a little girl in a beautiful black dress, playing with a new doll who was dressed in red. She was looking at the new arrival. If you listened closely, if you really tried, you might have heard a whisper – "Smile. The dead should be pretty."

Roads Never Traveled
(Dedicated to Kristy Walter-Olson for her birthday)

Fate exists. It's a winding, crossing, beautiful thing, and it exists.

Picture a lane or a walkway, stretching off into the distance. You walk down this path as time goes by, but the path isn't singular. It branches many times in countless ways to infinite other paths. In some paths you're rich and in some paths you're happy, but seldom are you both. As you proceed down your path, certain byways open – opportunities to change your fate. Turn left, it says, to go to school longer. You won't learn a lot more, but you'll meet more people, you'll live more, and that's important. But hurry up, the branches shift. Wait too long, and you'll be hit by a car in a crosswalk – your path will end.

If you pay very close attention, if you concentrate very hard, if you're tired enough, you can feel the path you're on, and you can feel the opportunities changing, and closing, and vanishing. The longer you wait, the more inevitable your life becomes, the less your path diverges: opportunities drying up like oases in the desert. You may begin to wonder if those other people, versions of you who made other choices, who were braver, or quieter, or less intelligent, are better off.

The kicker is this: there is no wrong way to do it, no wrong path to take (no matter how short), but then, there's no right way, either. There's just life, and the choices you make – millions of them a day, passing you by on your inevitable march to death.

Can you feel them?

The Visitor

A bored woman stood next to an ornate fountain outside of an office building, impatiently tapping her foot. It had a rhythm – every three seconds, *tap-tap-tap*. Just as she was beginning to think that what she was waiting for would never arrive, a younger, blonder girl walked up to her, bearing two cardboard cups with little plastic lids. The woman eyed them like wounded prey. "There you are, April!" her eyes darted from cup to cup, "Which one's mine?"

April shook her head and smiled. "You're a fiend, Irene, you know that?" but she relented and handed her one of the coffees, then yawned deeply. Irene wondered at the ever-growing dark bags under her friend's eyes, but said nothing. "I gotta run – early meeting today," April said, then turned to leave. Over her shoulder she called out, "Remember, it's your turn tomorrow," then smiled and walked away. Irene held her coffee cup in both hands and sipped the acrid, comforting liquid. She glanced at her watch and, reluctantly, decided to start work early and meandered to her office. She didn't notice the gentleman in the dark suit watching her from the lobby window, not when she walked through the glass doors, and not when she walked past him. Nobody ever does.

Irene awoke startled. The nightmares had been getting worse lately – more real, more tortured. She glanced around the moon-soaked room. Her bloodshot eyes told her that a man stood in front of her window, staring out of the thin curtains, basking in the light. She furrowed her brow and rubbed her eyes to attempt to dislodge the residual horrors of her troubled psyche, but the man remained. She trembled.

"Who are you?" she asked through unsteady lips. The man turned to her. She couldn't see his face, she couldn't be certain, but she could have sworn he smiled.

"Who am I?" he started, "Who are you? What is this place?" He sounded confused. Irritated.

"*This place* is my bedroom," Irene replied, indignation showing through her fear.

"Is it? I see..." He turned back towards the window, suddenly calm. "Can I stay?"

She looked at him curiously. Who was this man? Why did he seem so strange? Why didn't she want to scream or run away? "What's your name?" she asked. He turned to her.

"Well, that's the question, isn't it? For in a name lies the key to what one can become. Change one's name and one changes what one is; how one is perceived. So, I am forced to ask you, what *is* my name?" He stared at her in the darkness, holding her gaze without effort or care.

"I don't know," she admitted.

"Then how should I?" he turned to the window once more, dismissing her.

"What are you doing here?" Irene asked.

The man replied without turning around. "I thought it a nice place to be. It's raining outside, did you know?" Irene shook her head, then wondered why she bothered. "I like the rain. It makes me happy to be dry." He paused, "Pain, discomfort, annoyance, these things are important. Never give up what hurts you, it makes you appreciate what does not." His eyes followed a cat walking along the fence outside.

"What are you talking about?"

"About? Is a subject required? I was not aware... Yes. About. What am I talking about?" He closed the curtains, walked over to her bedside, and kneeled down, staring at her, taking long, relaxed breaths like ocean waves breaking on the shore. "Nightmares," he whispered, calmly.

"Are you insane?" she squeaked.

The man's laughter shook the very walls. "Oh, entirely. You would be too, had you seen what I have." He propped his head on an elbow on her mattress. "Do people miss them, do you think?"

"Miss what?"

"Memories. Do people miss them, when they are gone? Do they even notice?" he stared into her eyes, completely in earnest.

"I...don't know." She thought for a moment. "I guess they miss them, but only when they notice they're gone."

The man laid his head on the bed and ran his hand along the soft sheets as if every fiber were the most private parts of a lover. "Will you miss them?" he asked, absent-mindedly.

Irene gathered her knees to her chest, remaining under her ever-protective blanket. "What do you mean?"

The man's head shot up. "Ah! Another apt question!" He stood and went to the foot of the bed. "What one means is just as important as what one says. Even if what one says is gibberish, the *meaning* is pure." He looked at her, stroking his chin in contemplation. "Ack-sol, wind de bahbug?" he asked.

"What does that mean?"

He crawled onto the bed and positioned himself so close to her ear that she could feel the thrill of a secret in the gentle brush of his lips, and the horror of a stranger's touch. Softly, he whispered, "Will you miss them?"

Irene awoke the next morning, refreshed after a full night's sleep. She showered and got dressed for work in the usual mindless fashion. It was Tuesday, so it was her turn to buy coffee for her and April, and buy them she did. When she got to her office, she saw April standing in the usual spot next to the fountain, waiting for her. Irene approached and looked over her friend's haggard face while handing her their shared morning ritual. "You look awful today," she said with the bluntness of long friendship.

"Yeah, I've been having really terrible nightmares all week," April replied. "You know the ones where some invisible thing is chasing you? And you can't turn around, because you don't want to see it, but you know it's there, and it's... I dunno, hungry or something?"

Irene took a sip of her coffee and thought for a moment. "No," she said. Her forehead wrinkled in concentration as she reached out through an empty space in her mind. "I can't remember the last time I had a nightmare."

The strange sense of loss that she felt confused and irritated her. She was so wrapped up in what she could have forgotten that she didn't notice the gentleman in the dark suit walking away. Nobody ever does.

Drinking with Strangers

Drumbeat was a thug. Moreover, he was a thug's thug. He came up with clever ideas and plans which put his gang of thieves and, occasionally, murderers, ahead of the other gangs in the area. And he was having one of those days. You know the kind – they seem to backfire in every way whenever the opportunity arises. You tie your shoes and the shoelace breaks, you brush your teeth and you stab yourself in the gums, you shoot somebody and they just refuse to die. It was one of those. So, he decided he would do something that couldn't possibly backfire: he was going to drink until he was drunk.

It was a great plan. If he found, at any time, that he wasn't drunk, all he had to do was drink more, or faster, or switch to harder alcohol. It was foolproof. He drove to find a bar he'd never been to before, hoping to avoid familiar faces so he could really let loose and get so drunk that he'd forget how gravity worked. The place he found was a run-down shack of a dive away from any of the usual haunts where he would be known. He ordered a whiskey and soda on the rocks and took it to a dark corner booth where he could watch the locals try to get laid.

He was starting on his second drink when he saw a very lovely pair of legs attached to an even better ass walk in. The legs were wearing a loose black skirt and tall leather boots with thick soles that made them lean forward just a little. He watched them order at the bar, taking special notice of the girl's long dark-blue hair and the pale skin of her arms and thighs. Then she turned around.

He noticed her drink, something with orange juice in it, first, because he was the type of person who noticed what someone was holding before anything else. Then, because he has priorities, he noticed her chest – a white tank top covered bra-less breasts of a decent size, and all of it was covered with a black-cloth jacket. The jacket once had long sleeves, but those had been torn off at some time in the past, leaving only short frayed stubs and chains that hung down from the shoulder. Then, and only then, he saw her face.

She was gorgeous – the kind of pale that ancient Greeks would devote slabs of white marble and months of time to make statues of – with small features and a kind, innocent face. She had cute freckles on her nose and cheek bones, and the blue of her hair reflected in her almond eyes. She hated her freckles. She complained about them whenever she got the chance, Drumbeat knew. He knew because she was always with Skids, and Skids was always sure to show her off. It was his prerogative, being the leader of the only gang in the area who could compete with Drumbeat's own.

There weren't titles with Skids and her, no official declarations of love or ownership, but it was known that she was his. All of that was running through Drumbeat's head when she saw him and, to his surprise, smiled.

She walked over to his booth and set her drink on the table's edge in an obvious way. "You know, if you don't close your mouth, flies might come and lay eggs in it," she said. Her smile attempted to blossom into a laugh.

Drumbeat quickly closed his mouth with a dull *click*. He hadn't even noticed it was open. He took a drink to cover his embarrassment. "Where's Skids?" he asked, as rudely as he could manage.

"I dunno, at home, probably." She stood at the entrance to the booth for several awkward seconds. "Aren't you going to invite me to sit down?"

Drumbeat made a face, then waved his arm at the seat across from him. "What do you want, Sarah?" he asked as she scooted into the booth.

36

"Just some polite conversation. You remember how to do that, right?" Sarah retaliated. Drumbeat shifted uneasily.

"Does Skids know you're here?"

"No. He thinks I'm at my mom's."

"Fine," he sighed, "What do you want to talk about?"

Sarah laughed, "Let's start with what crawled up your ass and nested."

"Well what the hell do you want me to say? If word gets back to Skids that you were seen sitting with me, he'll start the wars again just to get to me." Drumbeat was careful to keep his voice down, and it showed.

"That's why I'm here. Nobody knows me here, and even if word gets back to him, I'm at my mom's place, remember? So calm the fuck down." She drained the something-with-orange-juice-in-it, then slammed the empty glass down on the table.

Drumbeat felt small all of a sudden. It wasn't a feeling he was used to, and he found he didn't care for it. "Alright," he said, then got up and left her behind, sitting in the booth with her arms crossed over her chest. He came back a minute later with two new drinks – one for each of them. "Sorry," he said.

Sarah smiled. "That's better." She took the drink from him and took a sip.

"You're awfully trusting," Drumbeat teased, "What if I roofied the drink?"

"I'd be mad at you," Sarah replied, calmly, and took another sip while looking him straight in the eye. Drumbeat laughed.

"So, what's new?" he asked.

The conversation went well. They each caught up with each other's lives, shared their triumphs and defeats, and proceeded according to Drumbeat's original plan. Between various trips to the bar for more drinks and even more trips to the bathroom to make room for them, each began to sit further into the circular booth on their respective sides. As the night wore on, it found them sitting next to one another at the back of the booth, shrouded in a private darkness all their own.

Sarah became quiet suddenly. She drew away when Drumbeat slid nearer to her, and seemed to withdraw into her own mind.

"Do you ever think of just... walking away?" Sarah asked, finally.

"What do you mean?"

"I mean, just... leaving. Just getting out, letting someone else run things."

"I can't. I've pissed off too many people along the way. They would come after me if I left. Hell, my own boys would come after me."

Sarah placed her hand on Drumbeat's forearm. "Are you sure?" she pleaded. Drumbeat nodded. "I see." She shook her head. "You're the only ignorant people on death row, do you know that?"

"What the hell are you talking about?"

"Sooner or later, you, Skids, everybody, you're all going to die. Does it really matter how? If you leave, maybe you could live a bit longer, or a bit better. Just, anything."

Drumbeat stared into his mostly empty glass of melting ice. "I just can't."

Sarah turned away from him and looked out a nearby window. After a few moments she turned back. She took a deep breath, and let it out in a long sigh. "Alright, dead man, so you don't have long to live. If you ask me, that means you can do whatever you want. I mean, the worst they can do is kill you, right? You're free." Drumbeat lifted his head. Their eyes met. She drew closer to him. "So what will you do with your freedom?"

Drumbeat leaned in and kissed her, passionately, deeply, her soft tongue entwined in his as they held each other closer than either had ever dared.

Drumbeat was the first to pull away. He leaned his forehead on hers and whispered, "I wish I could."

Sarah nodded, and teardrops shook loose and fell silently from her almond eyes, darkening her mascara.

They spent the rest of the evening in each other's arms, simply enjoying the closeness of one another. As closing time rolled around, they walked to the door, arm in arm. Before the door opened, Sarah pushed away from him and walked into the night, leaving him behind. Drumbeat shook his head, sadly, and walked out as well. Despite his best laid plans, he felt as sober as when he'd arrived, but the night seemed colder, somehow. It was one of those days.

Every Blank Canvas

"What is art?" the question hangs in the air, begging to be answered, knowing with smug satisfaction that no real answer exists.

"I don't know," the man replies. He stands in front of an easel, staring at the blank bit of parchment there, holding a dry paintbrush in a clenched fist dangling at his side.

"If you don't know, why are you trying to create it?" the words strike the man like a stiff wind on a winters day. He begins to tremble.

"I have to," the man whispers, "it's important." He lifts his brush and smears two colors together on his palette.

"Why is it important?"

The man stops.

"People need art," he croaks.

"The world has enough artists. It doesn't need more."

He sets his paintbrush in a nearby tray and picks up another, smaller one. "*I* need art," he admits.

"And what makes you so special?" The words wash over him. He takes a deep, unsteady breath, closes his eyes, and lets it out again.

"Nobody can create what I can create." The man opens his eyes. He puts down the second paintbrush and exchanges it for a knife.

"Of what use is art?"

He stabs into the top left corner of the canvas and pulls the blade diagonally across the field. "Art makes us think, and feel, and laugh." He plunges the blade in at the side and twists it, "It tells a story," he continues, "but hides the ending." He grabs a nearby stapler and closes the large wound in the canvas with it.

"Why would it do that?"

The man takes up a brush once again and mixes colors expertly. "Because," he replies, "it doesn't know what it will be."

The Price

Adam had started the day in the usual manner: wake up just before his alarm goes off, try to go back to sleep for those fleeting few seconds that remain, fail, coffee, shower, breakfast, dress, ponder life during his morning bowel movement, and go to work.

He had walked by the hole-in-the-wall curio shop many times over the last couple years. He worked just down the street from it. He thought of the curio as a strange remnant of a bygone age – a hanger-on of times when you had to visit a store to get oddities instead of simply searching for them online.

He passed by the curio shop with its wide front window and dark stone exterior, and peered into it. The bent old man who usually ran the place from his customary location behind the counter was nowhere to be seen. The big sign on the glass door read "Open" in several strange languages, and seemed to shiver and morph between them as he looked at it. Adam wondered for a moment if anyone ever actually went in – he certainly never had, and, glancing at his watch, saw no reason to break a winning routine.

He continued to his building and to his office on the sixth floor, taking the stairs because they were faster. When he got to his desk, two men in building security uniforms were waiting for him. The larger of the two looked up as he approached. "You're Adam?" he asked.

"I was this morning," Adam replied, more sarcastically than he had intended.

"Come with me, please." He held out an arm to proffer Adam the direction of the Human Resources Manager's office. The second man stayed behind. Adam glanced back as he walked to the H.R. office, and saw him unfolding a box and taping the bottom together.

The head of H.R. beamed at Adam with a well-used smile as he entered. "Good morning, Adam. How are you today?" He spoke as if it were the most important question at the moment, and had a slight lilt to his voice.

"I'm fine. Apparently you wanted to see me?" Adam had a sinking feeling that he knew what this would be about, and braced for it.

The head of H.R. took off his glasses and held them in one hand against his lips. They bounced as he spoke. "Adam, you're a bright young man, did you know that?"

Anytime now, Adam thought. Out loud, he said, "Thanks."

"You're what, twenty-six? Twenty-seven?" the glasses bounced.

"Thirty-two," Adam replied, curtly.

"See? Plenty young. Thirty is the new twenty, I hear."

Who keeps spreading that bullshit?

"Adam, we feel that we might be holding you back from your greater potential."

Ah, here it comes.

"So, we've come to the conclusion that the best course of action is to let you go, so you can be free to pursue your potential and grow to your fullest." The H.R. manager leaned back in his chair and smiled, putting his glasses back on. It was all so damn polite. Adam felt like he might politely punch this man in the throat.

"You're firing me?" he asked.

"Not at all. We're just setting you in a new direction."

"A direction that you'll no longer be paying me for." It wasn't a question.

"Exactly."

"So, you're firing me."

The man took off his glasses once more and set them, dejectedly, upon his desk. He sighed. "Adam, you

44

just don't understand. If you want to see it that way, that's fine, but we don't."

Adam was ushered out of the office and back to his desk by the large security guard, and found that the other had already emptied the contents of his desk into the box that now sat on top of it. After working there for nearly seven years, he had expected it to be a bigger box.

"We have to escort you off of the premises, sir," the guard said, handing the box to him, "It's just policy, nothing personal." Adam glared.

Outside, the springtime weather took a sudden turn for the dismal. *How fitting,* Adam thought, *fired and walking home in the rain. If today gets any worse I might have a hit country song.* He carried his box through the rain, belittling himself for not driving today with every drop of rain that ran down his face.

He didn't notice the box coming apart from the damp. A vintage dancing mechanical soda can was already halfway out of the bottom when he caught it. He glanced over his shoulder to see a trail of knick-knacks and loose change that somehow seem to breed (along with paperclips and rubber bands) in desks drawers. Then the box fell apart entirely. He watched as it slowly began to disintegrate in a shallow puddle.

He stared down at the rapidly-soaking papers, handheld games, pens, and other fairly useless things that were entirely, intrinsically, his, and sighed. He gathered the items, pocketed the change, and looked around in the hope of finding something to collect his work-life and found that luck had placed him in front of the curio shop. *Well, why not?* he thought, nudging his belongings out of the rain and under an awning with his shoe.

A tinny bell tingled a shrill announcement as he walked through the front door of the shop. "Hello?" he called out. The old man was still nowhere to be seen. "Anybody here?" He casually went about perusing the merchandise on the shelves. There were golden lucky-cats, sets of three monkeys roughly cast in speckled bronze, old plastic Godzilla dolls, mummified monkey paws in various states of decay, statues of videogame characters, and back behind it all, sitting on a disintegrating velvet cloth, the most amazing thing Adam had ever seen.

The box itself, for it was a box, was a dark green glass, imperfect and wavy, with small air bubbles embedded throughout. Inside was a brilliant spiral of white light, shaded green from the colored glass. The light seemed to change and fade as the spiral spun around the center of the box. Adam reached out to open the lid.

"Can I help you find anything?" The sudden voice from so close made Adam jump, hitting his hand on the shelf and knocking over a plastic bonsai tree. He turned to see the smiling face of the shopkeeper, grinning at him from a full foot below his eye level.

"Uh... yes. Well, I came in looking for a box or a container, but I saw this glass box back here and–"

"Don't touch, please. It's very fragile," the old man said, pleasantly.

"But, what is it?"

"A seed."

"A seed? For what?"

"Possibilities," the old man chuckled, "endless possibilities."

Adam glanced around the dusty shelves. "You've been here a long while, haven't you?" he asked.

"Oh, not too long."

"Do you collect oddities?"

"Some. Of course, many strange things turn up in a curio of their own accord."

Adam simply couldn't resist, "What are some of the oddest?"

The old man's smile broadened. He walked to the front door and turned over the sign hanging from it so that 'CLOSED' showed to the outside world, locked the deadbolt, and motioned Adam to follow him into a back room, hidden behind curtains and a threadbare tapestry.

The first thing he stopped next to was an old slot machine. The paint was chipped, showing the bare and dented metal underneath. The spinner was mostly blank, save for the faintest traces of strange and indecipherable symbols. The handle was a repurposed stick-shift. "What's this?" Adam asked when the old man simply stood next to it, grinning expectantly.

"It's a very special slot machine. It only has one pull left before the jackpot."

"Why don't you pull it, then?"

"Because it *always* has one more pull before the jackpot."

Adam stared blankly at the old man. His brow furrowed. He opened his mouth as if to speak, then closed it once more.

"Give it another pull, then," the old man conceded.

Adam shrugged, dug a quarter from his pocket, put it in the machine, and pulled the stick-shift...

The first thing he stopped next to was an old slot machine. The paint was chipped, showing the bare and dented metal underneath. The spinner was mostly blank, save for the faintest traces of strange and indecipherable symbols. The handle was a repurposed stick-shift. "What's this?" Adam asked when the old man simply stood next to it, grinning expectantly.

"You'll never know," the old man said. He chuckled to himself and moved on.

Next, he motioned Adam towards a broken headset resting on the decapitated head of a mannequin. It looked like a pair of flight-headphones from WWII, but parts of it were much older than that. "Will you tell me what this one is?" Adam asked.

The old man giggled. "It's a headset, and it tells secrets," he said, then giggled some more.

"Whose secrets?"

"All secrets." Adam was intrigued, and it showed. "Put it on, put it on!" The old man grabbed the headset and put it around Adam's neck.

Adam could pick out the harsh whispers of millions – billions of voices; all languages, all dialects, all volumes, all variety of voices whirled and warped together to make a kind of incomprehensible white noise which emanated out of the headphones around his neck. He hesitated.

"Go on," the old man goaded, "put them over your ears. It all becomes clearer, then." He smiled, pleasantly, and Adam put them on.

The noise blended, condensed, began to form one singular voice out of the multitude. It spoke – in wondrous volumes, it spoke.

Adam was still screaming when he awoke on the floor. The old man was calmly putting the headset back on the plastic head. "That must have been a doozey," he said.

Adam stared at the mannequin head, and imagined listening to that *thing* for so long, and shuddered. "I heard..." he swallowed with a dry mouth, "Is that real?"

"Only as real as you or I, but real enough, yes."

Adam suddenly got the feeling that this shop could be a very dangerous place – dangerous, but interesting. Curiosity outweighed the feeling that this was a place where truly anything might happen. So when the old man smiled at him once more, he couldn't help but ask, "What else?"

The old man's smile broadened as he helped Adam to his feet. They walked through the front room and past a mirror that Adam only noticed out of the corner of his eye, but his reflection noticed him much sooner, and followed him across the room with its eyes, biding its time.

The shop keeper stopped beside a closed door. The outside walls of the room were covered with mattresses tied to straw glued together with foam, anything to deaden the sound trying to get inside the room. "What's in there?" Adam asked.

"The Dreamer," the shopkeeper replied, matter-of-factly.

"Uh huh. And what's he dreaming about?" Adam's tone was skeptic.

"The universe, from the distant birth of stars to the daily decisions an ant makes. He dreams, and he creates, and he listens. He's not due to awaken for quite some time yet, but when he does..." the old man's speech was suddenly stifled, as if trying to avoid a lump in his throat.

"What will happen then?"

"He'll begin a new dream, and forget this one." His smile faded for the first time since Adam's arrival. He hung his head, looking older and greyer than ever before. Softly, he said, "Such is the way of Dreamers."

Adam looked at the old man, wanting to console him, to help him through his worries, but somehow he knew that The Dreamer must awaken, one day. He couldn't explain it, but he knew it to be true, and right, and absolutely sad.

When he came out of his personal reverie, the old man was smiling once again, as if nothing even the slightest bit unpleasant could possibly exist within the world. "What did you say you came in for?" he asked.

"Uh... a box. To hold my things," Adam replied, absentmindedly. The old man nodded, then went and dug in a pile of discarded baskets and strangely worn bits of cloth. He came up with a simple wooden milk crate and handed it to Adam. "Thanks. How much do you want for it?"

"It's free," the old man beamed, "so long as you come back again tomorrow."

Adam looked around the shop as they were walking through to the front door once again, glancing at the shelves and doorways he had yet to examine, and smiled. "You've got a deal," he said.

The old man saw him out, turned the sign back over to the 'open' side, and watched him stack his soaking belongings in the crate, and smiled.

The next day, Adam arrived bright and early to the curio shop. He was not at all surprised to find the shop already open, and the old man standing in his customary spot behind the counter, smiling. "Did your box work out?" he asked.

"Well, it certainly held all of my stuff from my old desk. The problem was, when I went to empty it, my stuff was gone."

The old man nodded, sagely. "I feared that might happen, but not to worry, you'll see those items again."

Adam helped the old man move things around the shop, organize a few oddities, and generally clean up the place for several hours. The whole time he was there, not a single customer came through the front door. Eventually, Adam spoke up. "Slow day?" he asked.

"Busiest it's been in years," the old man replied.

Adam laughed and continued cleaning. "This place must have a high rent for the space – prime location, busy street, downtown..."

"Yes, I suppose it does," the shop keeper nodded, looking around the shop approvingly.

"How do you afford it if you never have any customers?"

"I don't," the old man laughed, "I once gave the man who owns the space a one-of-a-kind artifact, and he's left me alone ever since."

"What was it?"

"Some old king's hand. Seems he had a strange curse put on him – his hand kept turning everything it touched into gold."

Adam stood and leaned on his broom. "Wait, you don't mean Midas, do you? *That* old king?" The old man nodded. "Somehow I thought it might be. And... *you* had his hand?"

"He wasn't using it." The shop keeper smiled, deviously.

"If it turns everything it touches into gold, what happens if the guy you gave it to drops it on the ground?" Adam asked.

"Well, I suppose the world would be much more yellow," the old man replied. Adam shook his head in disbelief and grabbed a large, moss covered stone from the floor.

"Where's this go?" he asked, then shouted in pain, dropped the stone to the ground, and ran around the room holding his hand by the wrist.

"I generally don't touch it, myself," the old man said, calmly.

"You could have warned me!" Adam yelled.

As the two bickered, the reflection watched. It began to mime Adam's movements, to mouth his speech. It only stopped when it noticed the old man glaring at it. In an instant, the mirror was empty once more.

"What are you so angry about?" Adam asked, coming from a back room with his hand wrapped in clean white cloth.

The shopkeeper turned to Adam, a smile replacing his scowl. "Just a memory, that's all." He looked at Adam's face for a moment, then, "Tell me, why were you carrying that box in the rain before?"

Adam picked up the fallen broom and leaned it against the wall. "I had just been fired. The box was just all of my desk junk."

"Ah, I see. So, you didn't come in here for a box, you came in because you needed a change, something to occupy your mind after a bad morning."

"Change? No, not really. I mean, maybe a little, but what's the use? I hated that job, anyway."

The old man came out from behind the counter. "Lock the front door for me," he said. Adam did as he was asked. "Tell me, how can I repay your generosity?"

"All I did was clean up a bit."

The old man looked at the mirror, and worry broke out on his forehead. "You may have done more than that." He walked to the mirror and took it off the wall. He set it face-up on the countertop, looking into it, but his face wasn't reflected.

"First time I've ever seen a mirror that didn't reflect," Adam said.

"It reflects," the old man replied, sadly. Adam came and peered into it, and sure enough, he saw his own reflection looking back at him. Only, it was a little behind. He would move, then it would move. It reminded him of a video that was out of sync with the sound.

"What the hell?"

"It likes you," the old man said.

Adam looked at the old man, once so cheerful, so perpetually happy, now broken down and sorrowful. He grasped the mirror and held it up...

And suddenly the mirror wasn't a mirror, but a window, showing the curio shop behind the glass. He saw himself stand up, turn, nod in gratitude, and walk out the front door. The old man through the glass picked up the mirror and hung it back on the wall, then sadly slunk away to stand behind the counter as the window went dark.

Adam smiled. He walked up behind the young man who was inspecting a box that once contained The Seed of Possibilities on the shelf. The box itself was now empty, but still had amazing powers all its own. "Can I help you find anything?" he asked.

Dead Men's Faces

If you would have asked her, at 25, how long she would live, she would have responded "I'll die at 97." Liz would do things like that – optimistic, but grounded in some sense of reality, fueled by an absolute confidence.

The craziest part about it is she would have been right:

Liz Maulding: dead at 97 years of age.

Of course, she was a little mad in the evenings (which began at 3pm at the latest), a little groggy in the mornings (4am, sharp), and downright cruel every other day, but it was in the last year that she began to go truly insane.

"The lights," she would say, "the lights aren't right." She would get up and pace around the room, staring into each lamp and opaque reflection while muttering to herself. When asked what she was looking for, she would simply reply, "Dead men," and shake her head, sadly. Sometimes she would laugh, confusing the orderlies that attended her.

It was during one of these random episodes that a visitor came to see Liz. He was a young-faced man with a limp, and followed her ritual with fascination – not unlike a child watching ants go off to war. He watched her shaking hand caress the glass in a framed picture on the wall, then go off to toy with the cobwebs in a corner of the room, all the while darting wistful glances at the dying sun through a cracked window pane. He almost smiled when she burst into a low, rumbling laughter.

The man walked up to Liz and sat down in a moth-eaten wingback chair next to her. "What do you see?" he asked her, his voice soft and pleasant. She smiled and weaved the cobweb gently between her fingers in intricate patterns.

"Cat's cradle," she whispered, and smiled. The stranger held out his fingers and took the pattern from her, and she in turn developed another weave by taking different strands from him, every iota of concentration poured into the action so as not to destroy the delicate web.

Suddenly her hand jerked to the left, stretching the brittle web to its brink. She took a deep breath and counted every single intricate knot in her design. "It's older than people think, this game," she said, and stared down at her cradle, holding it close to her chest as if nursing an invisible child within the folds of the disposed spider web. For a moment, it was as if the years melted away from her cracked and wrinkled form, and she was a young woman again.

The man reached down and clasped her hands together, crushing the cobweb into so much broken fluff. Liz only stared at her ruined effort, consciously ignoring a tear as it rolled down her cheek. Slowly she lifted her gaze to the man's smiling face. She bolted upright, thrusting the visitor's hands away from her. Such spryness one wouldn't expect from anyone even 20 years her junior.

She ran to the lamp and tore at the lampshade, her yellowing fingertips forcing the unlit bare bulb as near to her face as possible. Her eyes went wide and she dropped the lamp, moving instead to the mirrors, the picture frames, even the glare in the plastic tile of the floor. "They're gone," she breathed, "They're all gone."

She crawled on her knees to the window and stared into the western sky. Tears fell unheeded down her face and dried on the rotted sill. "Who is gone?" the man asked, knowingly.

"Their faces... They're gone." She stared at the deep red sky, unmoving, for hours, watching the last rays of the sun fade away. Her visitor, unseen and unheeded by the staff, kept vigil with her until the very end.

As darkness draped its cloak across the land, Liz Maulding gave up her last breath in a whisper, "Give them back..."

She was 97 years old.

The Four Letter Illusion

What is love?
Ask yourself that one question.
Think about it very carefully.
What is love?

You're wrong you know.
That's not it at all.
As a matter of fact, you couldn't be further from the truth
if you tried.
But now I'm being cruel.
After all, how could you know?

No parent will tell this to their children.
At least, no sane one.

A friend of mine says "Something like love is a breeze on
a warm summer day, and it makes you complete in
mysterious ways." He goes on to say "love is the stain on
the mattress when you put your clothes back on"
And he's right.

Not you though. Your absurd notions would have made
Socrates and Satan laugh in unison. Your idea would
have made the gods hate you for eternity,
But it would make your mother happy.

Would it surprise you to know that I've heard a lover
described as someone who beats you less than the others
do?
Are you shocked to think that love is something that has
been told to us so much, repeated so often, that we
simply believe it without question?

If you'd never seen an after school special about a boy
and a girl, never read Romeo and Juliet, never picked up
a romance novel, went through life deaf, blind, devoid of
physical feeling, would you know what love is?

Love is want.
Love is need.
Love is pain.
Love is pleasure.

Love is acceptance.
Love is revolt.
Love is whatever life has convinced you it should be.
That one unattainable thing.

That cold-light feeling in your chest.

That one piece of the puzzle you've been searching for.
Of course, you found it stuck under the couch, the
picture distorted, the edges frayed. It's so unlike the
shape of the hole in the puzzle of life that you've been
working on that you're not even sure if it will fit.

But it does.
Even if you have to force it in with a hammer, and hold it
down with glue.
It fits.

But your idea... that was just silly.

The Boring Man

An ordinary man: he got up at 6:55am every weekday morning. He got out of bed and, to save time, set his coffee to brew while he took a shower, where he soaped first his head, then his body. He got dressed in a business casual shirt and slacks, then sat on the edge of his bed and pondered calling-in sick that day.

He never did.

He poured his coffee into a travel mug, knowing that it saved him a few dollars a day over buying from a local café. He took that few dollars a day and saved it in a special bank account. He had quite a bit, now. He thought he might spend it on a cruise, someday.

On his way to his office job, he took the shortest route, always being in the correct lane for his destination well ahead of time, cursing those who cut him off at the last minute, but not loudly. He parked in his office parking lot at the first open space he saw, usually a few rows back from the entrance.

He got to his office building and greeted the front desk reception girl, a few years his junior. He gave her the same mildly-flirtatious-but-not-overtly-noteworthy banter that he always gave her. It was pleasant, witty, safe, and incredibly boring. She forgot about it as soon as he walked away, every day. He worked all morning, largely dealing with the papers printed from digital copies scanned-in from original copies that are themselves stored, presumably, in a black hole someplace.

He ate his lunch, which he made himself the night before and packed in a brown paper bag with his name on it and this morning put into the company fridge. When someone stole his lunch, as they occasionally did, he wrote unsigned passive/aggressive notes and taped them to the fridge when nobody was looking.

After lunch, he went back to his desk, chuckled under his breath at some of the pictures sent to him by coworkers, got very little work done, and went home. At home he cooked a modest meal with very little salt, watched the news, then went to bed.

To sleep.

And dream.

"John? Hey, is that you?" The voice is very near to him, and somehow knows his name, but it's not familiar. John lays still and doesn't bother opening his eyes. *Whoever it is will realize their mistake and go away*, he thinks. Then something hits him in the face.

He opened his eyes in an instant, ready to yell profanities at whoever hit him. He looked around his bedroom by the light of a nearby streetlamp shining through his closed blinds, but saw nothing out of the ordinary. He convinced himself it was a dream, even though his face still stung, and laid back down.

"It *is* you!" The voice is back, this time full of excitement. John opens his eyes and sees who's been calling him. It looks like a normal, slender man, only green skinned and with two small antennas growing out of his head. It reminds John of what a child would think an alien would look like. "Nobody had heard from you in so long that they sent me out looking for you. Took me months to track you down, but now I'm here! Everybody will be so pleased to see you!" The alien beams a toothy smile at John.

John sits in bed, confused. "Um... do I know you?" he says, calmly, then wonders why he's being calm. "What are you doing in my room? How did you get in here?!"

The alien rolls his eyes, "I've already told you why, as for how..." he points towards the closet door, "same as always."

"You came out of my closet?" John says, then looks at the near-glowing pink plastic tunic and blue vest the alien is wearing. "Fair enough."

The alien pulls John up by his arm, "Come on!" he says, "They're all waiting for you!"

"Who is?" but the alien doesn't answer. He drags John over to his closet and opens the door, then pulls him through. Inside is not the line of near-identical work shirts he is expecting, nor is the matching luggage set his grandmother had gotten him a long time ago sitting on the floor, still unused.

Instead, he steps out into a bright and joyful world. The sun rains down upon him like a warm spring day, birds play in a nearby pond, green fields and forests stretch out in all directions. And nearby is a picnic table, covered in all the most delectable treats he can imagine.

Around the table sits a giant pink bunny, a knight in full armor, a scantily clad witch, and a whole myriad of other creatures. "I found him!" the alien calls out. The whole group lets out a cheer as one and rushes over to the astonished John. Between torrents of "Where have you been?" and "We've missed you so much!" each creature or person embraces John in turn. Some even kiss him.

The last to reach him is the alien. "You've grown older," he says, smiling. "What game do you want to play?"

66

Suggestions come in from all around. A princess wants to play the dragon game, to which the knight heartily agrees. A mobster wants to play heist; a pirate, walk the plank. And a curiously fine dressed turtle in a tuxedo and wearing a monocle wants to play high-tea.

John has so many questions, like: "Where am I?" "Why is that turtle talking?" and, "Who are all of you?" but suddenly, something snaps into place and he remembers them all. He remembers all the games they would play, the magical rescues, the dramatic fights, the joyful abandon of just playing, all when he was a child. He would visit them, often, always when asleep – the people in the walls – and they would play until he woke up.

John smiles to himself as the warm feeling of Home comes over him.

"Let's play the dragon game," he said, his face suddenly cold as the alarm klaxon rang in his ears. His heart sank as he got out of bed. He started his coffee, he took his shower, he went into his room and stood, naked, in front of his closet door. He closed his eyes and threw the doors open, stepping through into a row of shirts and a pile of unused luggage.

With bitter disappointment he got dressed and went to work. The girl at the front desk was on vacation, an irritated old man informed him. After lunch, he emailed one of his friends in the same office, explaining the dream. His friend wrote back, listing off various psychological problems the dream could signify. John read it with interest.

That night he lay in bed for hours, tossing and turning with worry about his own mental state. *Am I crazy?* he thought to himself, *I couldn't be. I still go to work, I still bathe, and eat, and... shit, it's 4:32.* He rolled away from the red glare of his alarm clock. *But I don't remember being any different. Is that what it's like? Do you just exist from day to day and then, suddenly, you're insane? You go about talking to bunnies and aliens and... and... what was that other thing? I could have swore that I saw a panda.* He rolled once more. *It's 4:33.* He covered his clock with his pillow.

Work the next day marched on like an armored army through a bog. Lunch found John idly starring at an hourglass icon on his computer screen. A coworker walked up and prodded him in the arm. Jokingly he asked "Make any new friends last night?"

John shook his head. "I couldn't sleep," he replied, "some asshole got it into my head that I might be crazy." He glared. The coworker retreated, rolling his eyes.

"He's a rather dull fellow, isn't he?" the alien says, laughing. John turns to see the alien luxuriating across his desk, rolling the mouse back and forth, holding it backwards. "What do you think he gets up to when he's alone? I bet it's shocking."

John closed his eyes and rubbed them with the back of his hands. When he opened them, the alien was gone. Quietly, John wrote a note saying he wasn't feeling well and left it on his boss's door. He drove to his apartment as cautiously as he could, ignoring the princess who sits in the back seat and watches the scenery go by through the window. She was gone by the following stoplight.

That night, as he slept, he overheard a conversation:

"I don't think he's coming," said a voice.

"He'll come. He always liked this game. Besides, we spent all this time setting it up. How could he let us down?" said another.

"Maybe he doesn't like us anymore," the first whispered, sadly.

"Nonsense. We're amazing... aren't we?"

The voices drifted away.

John jumped up. "Wait!" he cried, then looked around his empty bedroom. His face was wet. *Tears?* He wiped them away. *I'm not crazy. I'm **not** crazy...*

The next day he went to work in his most comfortable shoes. He ignored the front desk girl, freshly back from her day off. She pouted as his back as he walked by.

He rode the elevator up to his floor and went to his cubicle, where he avoided phone calls and caught up on some overdue paperwork. The day sped by until the long awaited lunchtime arrived. He spread his arms across his desk and put his head down. With a smile on his face, he closed his eyes.

...and a half hour later, he awoke, refreshed, hungry, and absolutely miserable.

He swung by the drug store after he was off from a suddenly long day of work. Once he arrived at his apartment, he made a modest dinner, he watched the news, and then he went to sleep.

"So, the dragon game, was it?" the alien says, smiling at him.

They found his body four days later, still in bed, clutching the bottle of sleeping pills in his cold hand. He had a strange smile on his face. On the nightstand next to his bed was a note with only two words written on it:

Going Home.

An Evening's Ride

The deep orange sun set in a champagne sky. It shone brightly on the distant limestone cliffs that made up an impassible peninsula. The lower the sun went, the darker the sky and the lands below it became, until the world stood as if bathed in blood and darkness. Just as the last sliver of sunlight was about to be swallowed up by the night, time stopped. It stopped because it had been asked, politely, by a special guest, for a special meeting.

A man in white robes sat upon the blood soaked cliff, staring at the insignificant slip of sun that provided all of the light that still existed in this part of the world – just enough to see by, barely enough to be seen. He waited with the patience of a glacier, he had time, after all.

A window opened in the sky – a window the likes of which can be used to peer into a soul. It hung in the air without support and, through it, another world appeared. A world of dim shapes, where an idea has grave consequences, where a whisper can destroy galaxies. A face looked out from it, waiting, curious.

A shadow, an echo of a voice spoke from the darkness of the valley below the hill, as quiet as a storm, as gentle as a dagger. *You always did have a good sense of scenery*, it said.

The man in the white robes did not, dared not, turn around, not just yet. "It's just a matter of timing," he smirked, "Are the others joining us?"

I think not, came the reply, *I have not heard from them since the last gathering*.

The robed man turned. "Did you have another falling out?" he asked.

A faceless figure in a dark cloak emerged from the darkness of the valley. Its cowl bowed low and raised once more in a slow nod.

A foul wind blew in from down the hill – something that should have been impossible in a moment out of time. "He may not have seen me, but I've certainly seen him." The voice came from a frail, sickly man, who was marching along the crest of the hill. He looked as if he could scarcely survive such a walk, as if a sneeze or a stiff wind may render him unable to go on, but his eyes betrayed him. They were old eyes, accustomed to the troubles of life, and, indeed, the cause of some of them.

He coughed and wheezed through pale lips as he approached the gathering on the hill. When he reached them, he stuck out a disfigured hand as if to shake. The other two simply looked at the proffered hand, then at him. He smiled so broadly that several of his boils tore open and oozed fluids down his cheeks.

The white robed man bowed, and the sickly one bowed lower. "Welcome," said the white robed man. They stood and stirred in small motions, politely looking at nothing in particular. Again, the white robed man spoke, "So, it seems we are only one down."

The sickly man shook his head, then smiled. His yellow teeth looked darker still under the red sky. "He's been busy. He may not be able to attend," he said.

Why would he be busy? came the hoarse whisper from the dark cowl.

"He is *always* busy," the sickly man stated. The others nodded in agreement. They waited in silence for a time. The sickly man shifted from foot to foot on occasion. The man in the white robes leaned on his staff, alert and content. The creature in the dark cloak moved less than a mountain, neither bored nor caring.

"I like your work," the sickly one broke the silence, "You couldn't have picked a better moment."

"I know," the man in the white robes replied. There wasn't the slightest hint of pride in his voice, there didn't need to be, it simply *was*.

"Do you think–"

We do not speak of that until the gathering is complete! The dark-cloaked figure shrieked in a sharp whisper that caused the other two to stare. The sickly man contented himself to say nothing and enjoy the shades of red blending into the distant cliff.

The last to arrive did so at a stunted pace. It was obvious that this man had once been a massive, vital person, but the years had been hard on him. His large frame was outlined by scarred and tanned flesh, wrapped upon his bones like a snare drum. Each step took great effort. He seemed he may collapse from exhaustion, but on he walked, his bones creaking like an old cart wheel. The other three stood silent as he approached.

"Welcome." The white robed man bowed once more, "We weren't sure you would make it."

The frail, thin man just nodded in reply, still trying to catch his breath.

We may begin, the cowl whispered.

They all shared a glance between one another, none of them wanting to be the first to speak on why they had gathered here. It was always like that.

Finally, the sickly man cleared his throat, and spit an errant bit of phlegm onto the dirt. "Well, for my part, I think we should do it," he said.

"Why?" the thin man hissed, his breathing now closer to regular.

"The world is doomed. They once had me on the run, and I had feared that I would be eradicated, but in their avarice, they made me stronger than ever. It wouldn't take much to sew chaos among them, now."

A horse as sick and boil-ridden as its owner came out of a nearby forest in the valley, and obediently waited for its rider.

The black cloak nodded. *I, too, think the time has come,* its harsh voice sent chills down even such strange companions as these, but he continued. *They are many. There is a risk that they may simply out-breed my ability to be a real threat to them as a whole. Already, most of them know I await them at the end of their journey, but very few seem to care.* Its cowl fell. *I have nearly lost all that once made me great.*

Out of the forest in the valley came a horse so pale that it was normally nearly translucent, but now reflected the blood red sky, and seemed to be ablaze.

"I agree," said the thin man, reluctantly. He looked to the ground as if defeated. "They cannot support the numbers they have now. Their children starve, their elderly wither, uncared for. A slight tip of the scales would render them hopeless, their crops would dry up, and their water would be as poison. Doing it now would be a mercy. Now is the time."

A horse so thin that it seemed skeletal, each bone showing through its thin skin, suddenly stood next to the other two in the valley, in the shadow of the hill.

All eyes now turned to the man in the white robes. He was silent for several moments before he sighed. "Has the old argument finally come to an end, then? Have we made a decision?" The others stirred uncomfortably, not meeting the white one's gaze.

The thin man shook his head. "What choice do we have? If we do it now, we'll save them the pain of a long and drawn out end."

"Maybe you're right, but I feel that I must, unfortunately, disagree."

"Why?" the sickly man said, glaring.

"There is still a chance for them to survive. They are learning. I grant you that the possibility is so thin that even I can barely see it anymore, but like the sun beyond the horizon, the potential shines so very brightly against the darkness."

And stains the world with blood, screeched the dark figure, turning away from the others.

"If needs be," the white robed man agreed.

"Then it is settled," the sickly man said, then sighed, thinking of the long walk home. "I really would like to ride, just once."

We will, came the harsh voice, like grating steel, from the retreating cloak. *Until next time, brothers.*

A window opened in the nothingness, once more. The face in the clouds shook from side to side, disappointed, then vanished.

Time resumed as if nothing at all had taken place, for nothing had. And the sun set, only to foretell the dawn.

Morning Coffee

Two sugars and two creams.
No, that's not right...

He stares at the black abyss in the middle of a mug he and his wife had gotten from a dismal trip to Disneyland, where it had rained while they were in line and sent the locals running for shelter under hideously joyful awnings and shop windows. His wife had looked at him and smiled as people in the line gave up, one-by-one, and the line moved forward to the waiting rollercoaster ride. After the ride was over, the shops were empty – the anxious people looking to get their spots back for the rides. His wife smiled and picked out her mug with a triumphant laugh. He had always loved her devious side.

Three sugars and two creams, maybe?

Wafts of steam drift up from the mug and blend over a flower vase that his mother had gotten them on their wedding day. It's pink, with blotches of red and orange. His wife said it reminded her of a sunset on the beach. It reminded him of puking up orange sherbet ice cream mixed with cotton candy at the fair, once, when he was small. He had hated it immediately, and still does.

No sugar, just cream. No...

He notices, for the first time, a dark spot on the side of the mug in the middle of a chip on the rim. The chip evolves into a crack down the side of the cup, and he realizes that the contents are now steaming on the white tile countertop, leaving thin brown puddles in every imperfection. He stares at the intricate lakes.

Three sugar and four creams. That's it!

He grabs a washcloth from the sink and holds the cup in his hand while he begins soaking up the mess on the counter. He watches the off-white cloth turn a pale brown as it fills with the spilled liquid, then wrings it out in the sink. He's going back to wipe up some more when his eye falls on a picture frame next to the flower vase on the windowsill.

The frame holds a picture of his wife, smiling, posing like Vanna White next to the door of their first house together. He drops the cup and washcloth unthinkingly into the sink and picks up the picture frame in both hands.

He remembers the happy months they had spent in that house. He remembers the unhappy months of the disease.

He remembers the worst of all the days.

He sets the picture frame back on the windowsill and notices the time on the stove: 8:40am – his wife will want her coffee. He takes the curiously half-filled coffee pot from its own personal burner and fills up his wife's favorite mug, one they had gotten on a dismal trip to Disneyland.

Was it two sugars and two creams?

And Where it Stops...

Was that just a laugh? I heard it, I know I did...

He takes his headphones off and looks around the room. He's been busy with a computer game since he came home, and, living alone, nobody has complained, but laughter was something new entirely. It wasn't in his headset, but it was oddly familiar. He gets out of his chair and searches the room. Nothing is out of place, no long forgotten toy was giving its death knell, no precariously balanced object fell to make a strange laughter-like noise. The only sound is a high pitched ringing in his ears – damage from decades of listening to music too loudly and being too close to the stage at concerts.

He gives up the search and settles back into his chair. He puts the headphones back on and tries to get back into the game. A few moments later, a strange light from behind his computer monitor catches his attention – an odd, sickly green kind of glow. He leans over and peers behind the monitor, but there's nothing strange there. *What the hell?* He sets the headphones on his desk and shuts down the computer. "Sleep," he says, rubbing his eyes, "I need sleep." He meanders into the next room and gets undressed, then goes to bed.

Was that just a laugh?

He takes off his headphones, then hesitates, combating a familiar feeling and the odd tingling sensation in the front of his head. He ignores them, deciding to deal with it later, then gets up and looks around the room, searching for the source of the sound. The television is off, the stereo is silent, his phone lay dead next to his computer. *What was that? I know I heard something.* After a fruitless search, he turns back towards his computer to resume his game, but stops. There's a strange green glow emanating from the back of his monitor. He walks over to it, he looks at it, he smacks it, and then the strange glow dies away. *What the hell?* He stands there for a moment, staring at the back of the monitor. Finally, he grabs a screwdriver and unscrews the back panel. Inside it's... *wrong.* There's something off. It's fuzzy, distorted somehow, like it's–

What was that?

His head is pounding, so he doesn't bother standing up to investigate. He just looks around the room from where he sits, contenting himself with the idea that maybe he's running a fever, and imagined it. *Where the hell did this headache come from?* He lays his head on the desk and tries to will it to stop hurting. It's only by pure luck and accident that he's looking at the monitor when it begins to glow.

For the briefest of moments, there are two monitors, squished together like balls of putty. And where the two touch, an odd green glowing line is apparent. Then, the monitors are thrust together entirely, as if something bumped one of them forward into the other, and the glow stops. He glares at it. Whatever it was, it wasn't helping his head at all.

Suddenly, behind the monitor, he sees someone standing. They're slouched forward a little, holding a screwdriver. He can't see the other man's face, but he knows him, he's sure of that. He's about to stand up, when–

What the fuck!?

He throws his headphones off of his head. "Who's there?!" he shouts, "Who's laughing?!" He's tired of this. His head has hurt all damn night, and he just sat down to play some games and take his mind off of it, and now someone was laughing. His bloodshot eyes search the room, looking for the culprit. He gets up and crosses the room, trying desperately to ignore the onrush of pain and pounding in his head, every heartbeat makes his agony that much more unbearable.

He turns back to his computer just in time to see someone prying off the back of his monitor. "What the hell do you think you're doing?!" he screams. He runs at the other man and shoves him forward. The other man falls like dead weight against the monitor, skittering it forward just a little bit, then he vanishes.

He spots the other man again, this time sitting with his arm across his face and his head on his desk. He picks up the dropped screwdriver and thrusts it into the other man's skull. His headache becomes oceans of blazing pain behind his eyes. His vision blurs and his arms begin to shake. Then he sees the other man once again, kneeling, tying his shoe nearby, and once again on the other side of the room, throwing himself into the wall like a madman, and again, slitting his wrist with the same screwdriver that's buried to the hilt in another man's skull right now. Then he notices their faces, and runs into his room. He takes a deep breath. *It's not possible,* he thinks, but he throws on the light, and there he is, asleep in his bed, for all the world comfortable, and safe, and oblivious.

The pain in his head, the aches in his arms, the copies of himself all around the room, cause something to snap in him.

And he laughs.

Loud and heartily, he laughs.

Was that just a laugh? I heard it, I know I did...

Tentative

"Gather 'round, now. I have an important story to tell." The bent old man stares into the faces of the children sitting around him in a semi-circle, looking on with a mixture of admiration and contempt, unconsciously asking what this man could possibly have to say that was more important than climbing trees or picking fights with one-another.

"Before we begin, there is one thing you must all understand. Sometimes, Father Time, The Great Pace-keeper, and collector of incredibly large hour glasses, takes a break." He pauses for effect. "Now, you might say, that's not so strange. Everyone needs a break sometimes. And you'd be right, sure enough. But Time controls everything we do. Without Time at the helm, making sure everything happens in order and not all at once, you'd live your whole life in an instant, or have the worst headache for all eternity. He's that important."

The old man beams a benevolent smile at the gathered children. He knows he has their attention now. "So! He takes breaks, just like everybody else, but not quite. And not in the way that would give many dimensional theorists a joygasm, either." He trails off, quickly remembering who he's talking to. He glances around at the transfixed faces to make sure nobody quite caught what he said, clears his throat sternly, and continues, "But just think about it, the man has got to sleep sometime, right?

"Of course he does," he answers for them. "He doesn't require sleep like you or I, but he likes to dream, you see? As a matter of fact, he just took one. Just now, while you were sitting here, he spent ten thousand years exploring an asteroid belt that some idiot here on earth named with a lot of senseless letters and numbers. And that's a shame, too, because it has such a pretty name..."

He stares off dreamily for a moment, his audience sitting with rapt attention. "Anyway, Time took a nice, long break. And in all that time, not a single one of you noticed! Not one of you so much as blinked. Nobody in the whole of the universe, at least nobody wholly human, noticed it in the least. Oh, someone might have gotten a little light headed from the sudden jarring stop and just as sudden start of The Great Clock, but that's all. And besides, that could have just been gas, or heatstroke."

He smiles, a single tooth hangs from his gaping maw. "You see," he says, conspiratorially leaning in towards his listeners, "Chronos, by practice, is one of the most accomplished voyeurs in all the universe." He cackles. "Sooner or later, he can see everybody! At any given moment in your life, he just might choose to pay you a visit. But it is a lonely life, for he can never, ever, see you move. It's like a film reel going in slow motion. He catches scenes, moments, nothing more. And when he's not working, whether out to lunch or sleeping or some other tomfoolery, we all hold still like some kind of living gelatin out of a mold. We all stay pliable, again like gelatin..." He smacks his lips, and walks over to a nearby picnic table where he fills a plate with a wiggling mass of lime Jell-O with bits of fruit suspended in it.

The old man returns to his seat and talks between slurps of the slimy, flavorful substance. "So, Time wanders among us, completely ignored and alone, but that's alright. He gets back at us, you see. Have you ever been looking for your glasses, and you could swear they hadn't been on your head a moment ago, but somebody always has to point it out so everyone might laugh at your foolishness? And your keys, they are never quite where you could have sworn you left them, are they?" He chuckles to himself. "Time is a loveable scamp."

He finishes his plate, cleans it off, and places it back on the picnic table. He glances back at the group of children, still staring at the place he had been, towards a magician who stands there about to pull a bouquet of paper flowers from up his sleeve. The old man walks up to the magician and rifles through his sleeves, being sure not to disturb the magician himself. When he's finished, the paper flowers are up his pant leg, his trick cards are all in the wrong order, and his disappearing-water bottles are all filled with actual water. The old man smiles and nods at a job well done. As he's walking away, he remembers something suddenly, and snaps his fingers with the remembrance.

"Ta-D..." the magicians face goes pale as he brings forth an empty hand that he could have sworn had held the stem of his flower prop not a moment before. The gathered children all laugh at the man, who will only get more and more exasperated as the act goes on. A little ways away, a small dog is being scolded for getting into the lime gelatin.

Not far away, when-wise, an unbelievably old man chuckles to himself in a tired, half-hearted way.

A Quiet Drink

Samuel had just gotten off work. He knew his house stood empty and cold. The thought of going there after a particularly long shift seemed akin to drilling a hole in his foot to invent a lace-less shoe – pointless and painful. So, instead, he stopped at a rundown pub. Glowing neon signs told him to drink their particular brand of beer over the other, similar, brands of beer as he walked through the door.

He took a seat at the brass-railed bar. "What'll ya have?" the bartender asked, in a synthetic friendly tone.

"Whatever's on tap," Samuel replied.

He drank his beer in silence, not even making small talk with the bored bartender or the other tired patrons. They were the usual denizens of bars on an idle Tuesday – people who came to drink, not to socialize.

When he was on his third beer, the door opened and closed. Samuel didn't look up. Thundering, hollow footsteps approached and what might be a man took a seat on the stool next to him, and Samuel took a sip of his beer, quietly, intentionally, in an effort to ignore the newcomer. Then an arm covered in furs of dark grey, and white, and black thudded on the bar next to him. Samuel looked at the man.

Eccentric would be have been putting it very politely. The man had an immaculate coat made of various animals' fur, stitched together with thin strips of raw leather. A great black beard stuck out at all angles from his face, engulfing him almost to the rim of his plaid hunting cap. The thin slit between beard and hat turned toward Samuel.

"How's it going?" a gruff voice asked from somewhere within the hair.

"Could be better, I guess," Samuel replied, trying not to be rude despite his mood. "Yourself?"

"I *couldn't* be better!" the man replied. Teeth appeared within the hair. Samuel looked at them for several seconds before he realized it was a smile.

The bartender came and sat a shot of something brown and a mug of what might have been frothy piss on the counter in front of the newcomer, all without being asked. The man grasped the shot and tilted it towards his face, where it disappeared for a moment, then reappeared, empty. He then took a long pull from the mug.

"Ahhhh," the man breathed, "Nothin' beats a good beer." He turned towards Samuel, smiling cheerfully. "You know, in all the places I've been, not a single one has been without alcohol of some kind. Isn't that fantastic?"

Samuel shrugged. "Sure. Makes sense. Who would want to go through life sober?"

The man laughed and finished his beer in another long pull, then slammed it down onto the counter. "Barkeep!" he shouted at the bartender who stood only a few feet away, "Another boiler-maker, and one for my new friend here!"

Samuel perked up. "Hey, thanks," he said, and nodded his respect to the stranger. The bartender gave them their drinks.

The stranger grabbed his shot and beer, and turned to Samuel. "What do we drink to?" he asked, boisterously.

"To alcohol?"

Raucous laughter erupted from the stranger's beard. He tipped his glass to Samuel, and shouted, "To alcohol!" and they drank.

Three boiler-makers and an hour later, they were both leaning heavily on the bar top.

"...and two days later she sent the divorce papers," Samuel finished.

"Just like that? Took the kids and everything?" the stranger asked, genuinely interested.

Samuel nodded, then steadied himself from the momentum.

"What a bitch." The stranger looked around the room, now deserted save for the two of them and the bartender. It was the longest bout of silence to come from him since his arrival. "So, tell me, what's it like when one of your kind dies?" he asked, suddenly sober.

Samuel decided to humor him. "Well, some say there's a great big light, see, and some say there's this tunnel that you walk down. Then your spirit goes wherever you think it should, I expect." It was the least offensive answer he could think of.

The stranger nodded, sending his grey beard bobbing up and down. "My kind just...stop existing," he said, somberly. "That wouldn't be so bad, really. I could deal with that. But after we're gone, it's as if we never even existed. All traces of us just, *poof,* and gone." He shook his head and finished his beer. The bartender came over automatically and refilled it, then wandered back to the television.

"That seems like a silly way to die. I mean, what's the point?" Samuel blurted out, followed by a hardly stifled belch.

"Well, it's not all bad. Most of us live a long, long time. We're really hard to kill, once we take root," he drinks, "but I think it's my Time soon."

Samuel looked him over. "Nah, you look fine to me," he said.

"You think so?" the stranger patted himself about the chest and arms, "I dunno, I think I'm a bit too thin."

Inspecting his new friend once more, Samuel had to admit, he did appear a lot thinner than when he arrived. *But that's not right, is it?* he thought, looking over the patched and tattered fur coat. "How long have you got, do you figure?"

"A few minutes, maybe."

"That short?"

The stranger nodded.

"No wonder you're drinking."

The stranger laughed, only to be interrupted by a gravel-filled cough. "I'm glad to have met you," he said, holding out a gloved hand, "uhhh...?"

"Samuel," said Samuel, shaking the man's hand. It felt like bone beneath the leather of the glove.

"Samuel," the stranger whispered. He sat for a moment, finishing his drink, then nudged Samuel with his elbow, winked at him, and said, "Watch this."

It wasn't anything, really. Nothing spectacular, nothing dramatic. Just a quiet, sad, implosion. A little *pip* and a rush of air, and there was a furry, full bearded hole in the universe that nobody noticed.

Samuel drank his last beer in the same silence he had observed since he had arrived. He hadn't intended to get this drunk, or to stay this long, but for some reason he had just felt like ordering a bunch of boiler-makers. He thought he'd only had three, but there were six empty mugs and shot glasses in front of him. Maybe he drank more than he thought? He couldn't remember.

The whole place felt just a little off, now. But it always felt just a *little* off.

Night Terrors

It wasn't my idea at all to go to Europe. I hate traveling, always have. It was Gabs that made me go. She loves to travel and meet new people. Of course, she doesn't care who these people are, or what they might really want from her.

One time, when we were at a local bar, I got up to go to the bathroom, and when I got back she had a new drink in front of her. It was some fruity concoction with an umbrella stabbed through wilted fruit. "Where'd that come from?" I asked her.

"Oh, the bartender brought it over. That guy at the bar bought it for me. Wasn't that nice of him?" she replied. I had a mind to go up and start something with this dude, but he was there with three other guys. They looked like they could be half a starting lineup for a rugby team all on their own or the front page of a mug-shot newspaper. I decided to let it slide.

Gabs saw nothing wrong with it. She just figured the guy was being nice to her – didn't consider that he could have roofied the drink – didn't think maybe the guy was just trying to get her trashed. Some people always think the best of humanity.

But Europe? Europe would be worse. Gabs wanted to take a trip there the summer of our two-year anniversary. We both had some vacation time coming, and I had plenty of cash saved up from the overtime I'd been putting in at work. I wanted to go to the beach, stay in a nice hotel, get wasted and have drunken-freaky sex for a week, but Gabs kept saying she wanted to go to Europe. She talked about it like it was some fantasy world. I was against the idea entirely. I mean, spending that long on a plane, getting air-sick, finding people who spoke English, finding a hotel when we got there, converting money... it just seemed like such a hassle.

She came to bed in a particularly lacey bit of translucent nothing that night. I never could argue with her for very long.

So, after a week of planning, arranging our time off, packing, getting someone to watch the house and feed the cats, we left on a red-eye flight to a little coastal city in northern Europe.

Twelve hours later we landed, only to discover that our bags had ended up going the opposite direction and currently resided in Hawaii. *Well,* I thought, *that's a great way to start out our trip.* It must have shown on my face, because Gabs cuddled up next to me and told me not to stress out. She always knew how to make me feel better.

We caught a cab out of the airport and through the city during the evening. The cabby asked where we were from, and we told him. He asked if we had a hotel yet, and I told him we didn't. I immediately knew I shouldn't have been so honest.

"Well," he said in a deep baritone, "I happen to know of a hotel that would be right up your alley. My brother works the front desk there. Mention my name and you'll get a discount."

Gabs, ever the trusting one, thought it was a grand idea and told the cabby to take us there. I don't think she realized until we got into the hotel that the cabby had never told us his name, so we ended up paying full price. The room was a piss-smelling, cobweb filled catastrophe. Gabs loved it immediately.

"Look at that view!" she shouted, looking out on the city from our fifth floor balcony. I didn't look at the view.

"I'm going to take a shower," I told her, and went into the bathroom. I was still pissed-off. The entire situation was fucked up already, and Gabby just didn't seem to care. In fact, she was enjoying herself, and that annoyed me even more.

I stripped down and turned on the water in the stained tub. The water started out in a trickle – a deep, dark brown. Judging from the smell, it may have been hooked directly into the sewer. I sighed, and decided against a shower. I put my dirty clothes back on and walked out to the living room.

Gabs was on the phone. She hung it up immediately when she saw me come into the room. "You were quick," she said.

"Decided I would be cleaner without a shower. Who was that?" I asked.

"The front desk. I ordered dinner."

Dinner was a series of dishes that, I'm convinced, they only call delicacies to make tourists buy them, made of parts of animals you wouldn't normally find even in the worst of hotdogs, cooked in its own fat, or its own bladder, or, I could swear, its own feces. I ate sparingly. We were both tired after dinner, so we went to bed early.

In the middle of the night, I woke up. Gabs was sitting next to me, her back as straight as a board. "What's up?" I asked. She didn't reply. She just kept staring forward at a mirror above a chest of drawers on the far side of the wall. I looked at it with her, but I didn't see what could possibly be keeping her attention. I curled up next to her and laid her back down, but her head kept looking toward the mirror. "Are you okay?" I waved my hand in front of her face. Her eyes were wide open, staring. She looked horrified. "Gabs?" I shook her.

Suddenly she shrieked and bolted from the bed. "Gabs! What is it? What's wrong?!" I shouted at her, but she ignored me, still screaming with all her might. Then she stopped. Silence filled the room. For some reason, I had expected an echo. Barely pausing to even breathe, she ran out the door. I grabbed my pants and threw on a shirt, then took off after her, barefoot.

I got down to the front desk and rang the bell. The same greasy man who checked us in popped out from behind a wall and asked if he could help me. I explained the situation and asked if he'd seen Gabs, but he just looked at me like I was crazy, and said he hadn't seen anyone that looked like that come by here, but he had been at his desk in the other room, so he might not have seen her go by even if she did. I thanked him and jogged outside.

Various street vendors and other nightlife wandered the sidewalks outside the hotel. I asked one man, selling some sort of lizard cooked in its own skin on a stick, if he had seen her. He pointed down the street, towards a grassy hill. I thanked him and padded down the street as fast as my bare feet could carry me. I stubbed my toe after about a block, and it sent me sprawling into the side of a metal garbage bin. My toe throbbed, but I didn't have time to care. Gabs was in trouble, somehow.

I got to my feet and ran up the grassy hill. I wondered why nobody had built on this hill, since it was in the middle of the city. On the hillside, almost at the top, there was a small gated-off area. The wrought-iron fence guarded an ancient graveyard, and in the middle of that graveyard I spotted Gabs. She was in the same thin negligee that she ran out of the room wearing, facing away from me. I hobbled through the gate of the fence and tried my best not to step on any gravesites on my way to her.

"What are you doing?" I asked her. I could feel the tingle of sweat breaking out on my face and back now that I was standing still. My toe screamed for attention, but I still ignored it. Gabs was standing strangely. In a way, it reminded me of a marionette handled by an inexperienced puppeteer. I shivered as the sweat met the cold air coming in off the northern coast. "Babe? Come on, you're scaring the shit out of me," I pleaded.

Gabs turned to me. There were tears running down her face. "We made it," she whispered. She smiled at me, then. I began to walk forward, but stopped when my injured toe hit something. I looked down and saw a small circle of stones that Gabby was standing in the middle of. The stones seemed to be made up of volcanic rock, all jagged and at sharp angles. It reminded me of a mouth, wide open, with teeth pointing straight up at the sky. The thought sent a shiver down my spine.

I stepped over the stones and into the circle. Immediately, Gabby's features went from jubilant tears to monstrous rage. She glared at me with a face I had never seen before. There was hatred behind her eyes.

100

"Get out!" she screamed at me. I walked forward to her and put my arms around her waist. She let out a high-pitched shriek and clawed at my face. I jumped back to avoid her nails and fell back onto the stones, dislodging a few of them in the process.

When I looked up, Gabby was on her knees, digging at the soil furiously. I made sure I stayed out of the circle, and came and knelt down beside her. I reached out and put my arm on her shoulder, but she shrugged it away. "What are you doing?" I asked again. She ignored me as if I hadn't spoken. I had to restrain myself, watching her as she plunged her fingers into the soil again and again. It took me several minutes to realize she was digging in a pattern. It was the Omega symbol, but with strange differences.

She clawed five lines from the Omega to each of the nine stones that made up the circle, plunging her broken nails into the dirt with a savage haste I didn't know she was capable of. She picked up the stones I had knocked out of the way and planted them exactly where they were before, tilting the angle of the edges to gain some sort of shape that I couldn't fathom. When she finally finished, she turned to me.

I backed away in horror at what I saw. Her face... her face was gone. Her button nose, her slightly slanted eyes, her kissable lips, all covered-over with featureless skin. But somehow I knew, I just knew, that she was pleased with herself.

The symbol etched into the ground started to faintly glow then, and Gabby, or what was once Gabby, began to twirl around like a little girl who was discovering the joy of dancing for the first time.

"Gabs?" I asked. I couldn't look away. She spun faster and faster, planting her toe into the bowl of the Omega symbol. I heard laughter on the air.

In a flash, she was gone. I was alone in a graveyard at the top of a hill, barefoot and bleeding, dirty from falling on the ground, staring at a vacant circle of nine volcanic stones. I walked forward, into the circle, but nothing happened. I hadn't really expected anything. The woman I loved had gone insane and *something* had taken her place, then had vanished before my eyes. I began to cry.

I woke up in the hotel room, alone. I bolted upright in bed and looked into the mirror. It was angled slightly, and in it I could see the reflection of the hillside, and the graveyard. I made up my mind immediately, jumped out of bed, and got dressed.

I ran out of the room and out of the hotel as fast as I could past astonished street vendors and the nightlife of the city. I ran up the hill and through the wrought iron fence, passing over gravesites without caring to avoid them this time. I didn't have time to care.

Then I spotted the circle. I fell to my knees and desperately tried to scratch the shape of the Omega back into the soil. I plunged my fingers into the damp earth like a man possessed. When the nails on my fingertips peeled away and began to bleed, I took no notice. I had to try. I had to get to her, wherever she went.

102

When I was satisfied with the shape of the symbol, I began to trace the five lines to each stone. Somehow I must have knocked some of them from their place, because I had to position several of them back the way they were. Finally, I had it all perfect. I stood up and inspected my work. The symbol, the lines, the stones, they were all as Gabby had made them before. I smiled. This had to work.

I began to spin, madly. I planted each foot carefully, throwing myself around and building momentum. I ignored the feeling of nausea, Ignored the dizziness, I just spun faster and faster. I looked out over the city, watching the lights blur and streak together in my frenzy. Then, as I watched the light, I saw her. She ran forward to me, and clasped her hands over her lips. She was crying – shouting my name, but it was too late. I couldn't stop now. The symbol began to glow.

I hate traveling.

Sunset

It was sunset.

This one was something special, as far as sunsets go. It had pinks, and oranges, and reds, bleeding to a soft and darkening purple, fading to a deep blue shroud. Rays of light emerged from behind dark clouds, mountains lined the distance – it was perfect.

My day was less than perfect; less than great, in fact. It wasn't even close to good. I drove down the highway in a trance, moving quickly, far too quickly, not really noticing my speed. I parked in the designated visitor's lot and entered the front doors of the hospital. I entered an elevator and hit the second floor button. The random colored lines and oddly placed triangles that decorated the wall did nothing to improve my mood.

The elevator rose, the doors opened, and I followed helpful black-lettered signs to the Intensive Care Unit. The sun was below the horizon. As I glanced at it through the window, illuminating the world in a pale facsimile of itself, clutching at the mountains in a desperate attempt to remain. It would soon be dark.

Intensive Care was a work station encircled by a counter. Three hallways lead away from it in different directions. Rooms with patients in them dotted each hall. A nurse stood behind the counter, looking at papers with a glossy stare, shifting them between her fingers. I approached her.

"Excuse me?" I said, "Can you tell me where 217 is?"

She looked up at me, sniffed, rolled her eyes, and tilted her head in the direction of one of the hallways. "Read the signs," she replied. Later, I would wonder why she was so rude, what kind of day she could have had that would excuse her behavior, but not just then. At that moment, I was simply angry. I stomped down the hall to room 217, waking some patients who had been sleeping peacefully. Later, I would feel bad about that, but not just then.

Room 217 was quiet when I peered in from the too-clean hallway. It was a double room – two beds separated by a thin curtain. I shuffled around blindly in the dark, wondering which bed was hers, unsure if she was in this room at all, or if she'd been moved again, and nobody had thought to tell me. She'd had a single the last time I had been there.

"Hey," came a quiet voice full of pain and misery – her voice. I stumbled toward it.

"I can't see shit," I blurted out, then laughed. A lamp came on next to her, casting friendly orange light on the room, the curtain, and her beautiful face.

She was pale, but then she had always been pale. Dark bags that didn't belong to her had made a home under her eyes. Her lips were un-rouged and barely evident, splashed with crusted blood and cracks, all residing there as memories of their usual deep color. Her dyed green hair, as always, was a steep contrast to her features. She was gorgeous.

I leaned down and kissed her forehead. She smelled like the room did – all anti-septic and wrong, somehow. Her hair was a mess. I didn't look at it directly, I knew how much she was conscious of it, and hated it. She wasn't vain, not really. She simply took great pride in how she looked, and it showed.

I stood there a long time, unsure of what to say, then, "Did you catch the sunset?" I ventured.

She smiled and shook her head. It rustled against the pillowcase. "No," she replied, "wrong side of the building, but I'm looking forward to sunrise."

I smacked myself in the forehead with an open palm in mock-stupidity that I did not mock-feel. She laughed. She had the best laugh – a cross between a teenager's gleeful giggle and a joyous chuckle, and so very warm. It had always made me smile. I grinned like a fool at that one.

"How's Rodent?" she asked. She didn't want to get serious either, it seemed. Rodent was our cat: a great, grey, mangy thing with as much personality as the both of us combined. She named him Rodent because when she saw a creature tucked behind a dumpster, soaked to the bone, she had thought it was a rat. Then it had meowed at her, and she took it home. It lay in her lap the whole car ride. It still sleeps nowhere else.

"He's alright. Lays on your pillow at night. Misses you, I think," I replied.

"Awww."

I didn't tell her how much I missed her. "What was on the menu tonight?" I asked.

She counted off on her fingers. "Something grey, something white and mushy, and something green and wobbly. I ate the green bit." She smiled devilishly. I smiled back, but my heart wasn't in it. I found myself wondering why she didn't eat more, why I had to go to work to keep money coming in when I would trade the world to be by her side – why this was happening.

Someone cleared their throat. I turned to see a doctor framed in the light from the hallway. He waited there, patiently, holding a chart against his thighs in expectation. "I'll be back in a sec, babe," I said. I leaned down and kissed her rough lips, then walked into the hallway.

The doctor held out his hand. I looked at it for a moment before I shook it. "Having a pleasant evening?" he asked automatically.

I simply stared at him, wondering if anyone ever answered in the positive in an Intensive Care unit. "How is she, doc?" I dared.

He told me.

"Well, that about sums up how my evening is, don't you think?" I turned and went back into the room without waiting for a reply.

She was sitting up in bed, reading a "Get Well" card from her friends and coworkers. One of those mass-signature cards that everyone writes one line in, except for one person who pulls a John Hancock and fills up a whole side all on their own, right next to the one who is delightfully insulting. She smiled and set it on the nightstand. "So, how am I?" she asked, pointedly.

"You'll be out of here in no time."

"Uh-huh." She eyed me suspiciously.

"No, really, they're tired of hearing you complain about the cooking," I laughed. She glared at me, but smiled in that *I'm mad but that was still funny*, kind of way, in spite of herself.

Then we talked.

We talked about Rodent and his daily quirks. We talked about her coworkers and the one who did the clever insult. We talked about her parents. We talked about the garden patch that we never really took care of, and what we should plant so that we could ignore it for most of the season and still have something to show in the fall. We had little nothing-conversations about things that never really mattered and always meant more than anything else. We held each other.

When the sun began to rise over the horizon, I pulled her bed against the window. We cuddled and made drawings out of the white stuff left on her food tray as we watched the sun rise.

At five, I held her tighter.

At seven, I called in sick to work.

At ten, the doctor came and told me that I had to come back later so that she could get some rest. She threw a bedpan at him.

That evening, as I left the hospital, I walked by the same grumpy nurse from the night before. She looked at me for a moment, then quickly looked away. I got to my car and sat down in the driver's seat. I don't know how long I sat there, just staring at the steering wheel, but when I became aware again, it was already dark.

The sun had set, and I hadn't even noticed.

A Trip

I can never seem to get to sleep the night before I have to be up early for a big event. I'm a natural night person, so my brain resists an early shutdown. Instead, it runs through all the ways that the next day can blow up in my face as some form of revenge for making it bored.

So, on the day that I was due to drive from Portland, Oregon to Seattle at four in the morning to help a friend of mine move, I found myself already exhausted from being awake for the last twenty hours. On top of that, due to some complications, I had only gotten two hours of sleep the night before that. It had been one of those weeks. I had some coffee when I arrived, to take the edge off, then proceeded to fill a van with all the heavy bits of furniture, plus a smaller car with other various essentials in boxes.

We began the drive around 7:00am, me in her parents van, her in her car. We hit some moderate traffic, and drove straight through to Seattle, making it there around 10:00. So far, so good. I hadn't even swerved.

The place she had chosen to live via online ads was a run down, shoddy-looking house, with two odd men as roommates. The first couldn't stop twitching, and the second was a wide man whose shirt never quite seemed to reach his too-tight shorts.

We unloaded her car into her new room and discovered that the floor in the corner was sinking. Evidently a floor joist was rotted away in that corner of the house, which let the floor sink down to the soil beneath it, leaving a foot square area that would attempt to swallow you if you stood on it. My friend seemed unperturbed, and unpacked a couple boxes while I busied myself playing with her ever curious kitten, who promptly got bored, as cats do, and fell asleep on my lap.

My friend and I got to talking, and decided that I should play the part of the "Scary Friend" to keep her roommates in line. I did my best tough-guy routine by lugging awkward and heavy boxes and furniture from the van by myself while they watched, and by being generally surly and rude. My friend was so impressed with the act that she thought I should do the same to her boyfriend, who we were to meet later that night. I enjoy people being needlessly afraid of me, so I figured, what the hell?

We spent the day driving around, getting lost, and making fun of people who we passed. It was a blast. Eventually we returned to her new place and assembled various shelves she had bought for her room, and laughed at her grumpy, tired kitten.

It was around 8:30pm when we heard from her boyfriend: he would meet us at the movie theater. Then he called back to say he wouldn't. Then, he texted to say he would meet us for food, then he would meet us for the movie again. As their disjointed conversation continued over the phone, I busied myself by snooping through some boxes.

Finally, a decision was apparently made, and we left. My friend complained of her boyfriend's lack of ability to make a decision, and I laughed. I verified that I was to do my tough-guy act, and she agreed I should.

Her boyfriend, as it turned out, was a bit of a giant. I'm six feet tall, and he was a full head taller than me, and probably used to being the intimidating one in the room. I briefly entertained the idea that I should just act normal, but was entirely too tired to care, so the Scary Friend I was. He was nice, even bought my ticket for the movie, but I proceeded to be rude and a bit of a douche because, to my sleep-addled mind, a plan was a plan. The movie, which was three fascinating hours about dreams within dreams and how to lose oneself in one's own mind, played out without incident. I quite enjoyed it.

Afterwards, they made plans to meet later, and I got a ride back from my friend to the van waiting outside of her new house. She and I talked a while, but by that point I was beyond entirely exhausted, so I rambled on aimlessly on topics without meaning, ignoring the fact that she had made plans, and her being too polite to stop me. I vaguely remember giving what I thought at the time to be sage advice about life and people, but what was probably complete shit, and doubtlessly made no sense at all.

She tried to talk me into staying in Seattle overnight, she could tell how tired I was, but I had been playing the tough-guy all damn day, and I think it went to my head. I hugged her goodbye, she thanked me for my help, gave me some money for food on the way home, and I left.

I made it to the freeway easily and settled back to listen to odd music stations that I was unaccustomed to, and constantly fiddled with the dial to find songs I enjoyed. It wasn't long before I was nearly alone on the road. That was the moment when I discovered my van was shooting black laser-beams out of its headlights.

It was the most curious thing, it even had a fun sporadic rhythm. I had to keep looking further ahead of me to see what it could be shooting at. Then I saw it: a turn in the road and a gas station just a ways off of it. My van was trying to blow up a gas station. It was ironic. I laughed, loudly, to hear myself over the radio noise, but the gas station never blew up. I decided it was shielded, and told the van it would get it next time.

A few cars came onto the road after the gas station, which was exciting. I prepared to dodge the smoldering debris from my van attacking the cars, but to my everlasting disappointment, it had run out of power for the lasers, and had to recharge. I looked at the tail-end of an old pickup in front of me, and it gave me a buck-toothed grin in return. "Cocky bastard," I said, "He knows I'm out of power." So I sped up and passed him. It was then that real tragedy struck.

The car now in front of me was a small blue economy car, but that was only part of the problem – that economy car was so very sad. It looked at me with its squinty red eyes and frowned, its lower lip hanging almost to the road. *Why is it so upset?* I thought, *It's driving, don't cars like to drive? What kind of terrible life does it lead that it could possibly be so incredibly down?* I felt for that car. I even got a little choked up, and for a few minutes I really think we bonded.

I was horrified when my van, in a jealous rage, started shooting its evidently recharged black lasers at it. I changed lanes just in time, and drove a ways ahead. The sad blue car fell behind. I watched in the rearview mirror, my heart full of pity for that tragic vehicle, before it came to an exit and left my life forever. Sometimes I still wonder if it's alright.

Then, because it's the Pacific Northwest, or because the fates like picking on me, it started to rain. Suddenly I discovered that the van's headlights were far too dim for this kind of weather. When I started hitting the drunk-bumps on the side of the road because I couldn't see my lane, I turned on the brights. It wasn't much better.

The other cars were all a ways ahead of me by that point, and my van no longer felt threatened by any of them. I changed the station several times, cycling through religious talk shows and strange static, until I found a song I recognized.

And then I screamed.

A dragon! A massive red dragon was coming right at me! It took me a moment to realize that I was still driving, and thus moving towards it, instead. It had taken up roosting on the bottom of an overpass that lay ahead of me, and it watched my van approach. I could see its talons stir and its wings unfurl as I grew nearer. It was going to attack me, I just knew it, but the road went straight at it and I couldn't turn away. I was certain that I was going to die, and with absolute terror flowing like ice in my veins, I floored the accelerator. I thought of the sad car I had passed, and was thankful it wouldn't get picked off. My van went under the overpass...

...And miraculously came out again. I cheered with joy, and looked back in my mirror. The red dragon had missed! It lay broken and injured on the wet pavement behind me. I gave it the finger in celebration.

Then I remembered the money my friend had given me, and pulled off the freeway at the next exit and into a convenience store parking lot. I was still thrilled. I told the man behind the counter all about the dragon on the freeway, and that he didn't need to worry about driving home that night. He, rather rudely, suggested that I buy some coffee. I told him that the money was for food, but he said he would only sell me coffee, and that if it made me feel better, I could chew the coffee before I swallowed it. Well, that made perfect sense, so coffee it was.

I left the store and got back on the freeway, taking small sips of my too-hot coffee, and then the oddest thing happened. As I grew less tired, I started to doubt my own sanity. I couldn't have seen a dragon, surely. It was just a reflection of tail lights in the wet road. And the lasers, that must have been patch-tar. My eyes had been playing tricks on me, the damn things! I couldn't trust them.

I made it back to Portland and dropped off the van, still certain that I must have been hallucinating a little, and I laughed. I got into my own car and proceeded to drive home, hitting just the beginnings of morning-work traffic. I was overjoyed when I saw the car in front of me was a happy little hatchback. Its smile was above its eyes, but it didn't seem to mind at all. I was sure, everything was going to be okay, now.

An Unexpected Outing

"How much further is this place?" Mary, the young girl in the passenger seat of a stylish car, asked. Her date for the evening, a young executive-looking man in a smoky black suit, laughed.

"Are you getting impatient?" he asked good-naturedly, teasing. She smiled.

"I'm just bored. How long have we been driving?"

"About twenty minutes. We're almost there."

"This place better be worth the trip, is all I'm saying."

The man, Luke, laughed again, "I promise you it will be like nothing you've ever seen."

Mary crossed her arms and looked out of the window, staring into the darkness.

"What, out in the middle of nowhere? I've been to the boonies."

"Not at all," Luke replied, "In fact, it's in the middle of everywhere."

Mary shook her head and rolled her eyes, then closed them and stretched luxuriously.

"We're here," Luke said, suddenly.

Mary opened her eyes and looked out at the simple wooden building. There were worn cedar shakes lining the outside walls and a sign towering above them on a rusting pole that could have been from the 60's. On it were the words 'The Fire Pit.' It had little iconic flames painted along the bottom. "It doesn't look like much," she said, grumpy already.

"Don't judge things by appearances, it's bad form." Mary scoffed and thought about texting a friend to come pick her up, but found her phone had no service. "You haven't seen the best part, yet. Come inside." Luke got out of the car and opened the passenger door for her. He offered his hand, but she ignored it, using the door to help her stand up from the low car instead.

"If this is some hick bar, I'm so going home," she said, heading for the front door. Luke opened it for her. Inside was a small square room lined with thick black curtains that seemed to absorb the light from outside. A man wearing stereotypical voodoo makeup sat behind a wooden podium, reading an obscure magazine. He looked up.

"Membership card?" he asked, and held out his hand.

"She's with me," Luke said, calmly stepping forward. The man went from boredom to dogged attention in a flash.

"Of course, Sir, er... Lord." He smiled, his teeth stark white against his patterned makeup. He stood and peeled back the curtain, bowing low as Mary and Luke walked through. Mary was impressed.

"Lord?" she asked as they walked down a black velvet hallway.

"It's just a sign of respect, my dear. Don't make a big deal of it," Luke replied, nonchalantly, then smiled.

The hallway took a sharp turn then opened into a dimly lit, crowded room full of sweet scented smoke. The only really well lighted area was the bar itself, and Luke steered Mary through the crowd, heading for it. Mary fancied that the others in the crowd moved out of their way even before they got there, then closed back together again behind them.

The bartender was nowhere in sight, so Luke reached out and knocked, rapidly, on the bar-top. "Brace yourself," he said, looking at Mary.

From a back room emerged a huge man, easily eight feet tall and half that wide. Then she saw the man's face.

Luke's hand shot out to stifle her oncoming scream. "Don't do that," he cautioned, removing his hand from her mouth.

"But he's... he's..."

"Working. Be polite, Mary."

Mary looked at the giant man behind the bar, with his huge, gnarled horns, his long goat's beard, his coarse, hairy face, and huge, intelligent eyes. They were watching her. "What is he?" she whispered to Luke.

"A bartender," Luke replied, simply. "Gregory! How's your night going?"

The beast looked at Luke and made what might have been a smile. "It's going well, sire. What'll you have?"

"A top-shelf martini, I think, extra-dry. And the lady will have...?"

He nudged Mary, good naturedly, and she snapped out of the world her mind had been occupying for the last several moments. She looked at Gregory once more and suddenly wished to go back to it. "What? Oh, I'll have a uh... lemon drop?" The bartender nodded his great mound of a head and turned away to make the drinks. Luke looked to Mary.

"I told you it would be like nothing you've seen," he said with a flair, then smiled. Mary spun away from the bartender and took a deep breath. Leaning back on the bar, she looked out at the crowd.

"Where are we?" she breathed.

"Twenty minutes from everywhere," Luke said, joining her taking in the room, "You have questions?"

"So many," she replied. Luke laughed.

Mary examined each group individually, focusing on each in turn. She saw something... hairy, in the corner. There was a chess board in front of it. "What is that?" she asked, pointing. Luke turned his head.

"A simple Lycanthrope – a Werewolf, if you wish to be archaic."

"He's playing chess?" A piece on the opposite side of the board moved seemingly of its own volition. "...by himself?"

"What? Don't be silly. He's playing a ghost." Luke narrowed his vision at the table. "Charlie Chaplin, it looks like."

"He's playing chess with Charlie Chaplin?" she blinked, "Can you introduce me?"

"And interrupt their match? Wouldn't dream of it. Besides, on second glance, it may be Groucho Marx. I always get those two confused for some reason."

Mary shook her head in disbelief, then scanned the crowd once again. She paused on several very short people standing under a table. One of them pulled out a small pick-axe and struck the wall with it, peeling back the wood paneling. "Dwarves," Luke answered her coming question before it was asked.

"Don't they prefer 'little people'?"

"Actually, I think *they* prefer human beings," Luke laughed, pleasantly, "But these are actual Dwarves. They're never comfortable with such high ceilings, so they get something over their heads as soon as they are able."

Mary looked up to see how tall the ceiling could be, but her search was fruitless – there wasn't one. There was just darkness, and silence, forever. She shivered and took hold of the brass bar rail, just in case she started to float away.

The bartender set their drinks down on the bar, then turned to leave. Luke spoke over his shoulder, "Gregory, are you deliberately trying my patience?"

"I'm sorry, Lord. We are out of the good gin." The great beast demurred, to Mary's surprise.

"I see." Luke turned to him, but caught Mary's eye. "Very well," he smiled, "Be more careful next time, Gregory. I would hate for you to get into... trouble." There was blood in those words. The bartender somehow managed to make his great bulk slink away, moving to a strange tentacled creature down the bar.

"You must be important," Mary observed, moving closer to Luke.

"Hardly, I just...uh-oh. Mary, don't look at the...oh."

But Mary was already staring at the entrance of the room, shaking nervously. Luke quickly stepped between her and the figure cloaked in shadow that stood in the doorway. Mary turned her shattered gaze to Luke's face. "I felt... so cold. Like there was a deep hole – a void. Just... empty. And I was leaning over the edge, staring into it. Just a whisper, a breath, would plunge me into it, and I would fall... forever. Alone." A single tear fell down her perfectly made-up face, trailing mascara.

Luke embraced her. "I had no choice. I couldn't turn away. I had to..." She shivered in Luke's arms.

"Sorry about that. I was hoping he wouldn't be here, tonight."

"But what is he?!" Mary closed her eyes, tightly, and cried. Luke held her close, petting her head.

"That's an old business associate of mine. He's never given his name." He looked around the room for a moment. "It's okay now, he went into the pool room."

Mary grasped her drink and chugged it down in one swallow. She pointed to the now normal-seeming bartender, then to her drink. Gregory nodded. She turned back to Luke, her face a mask of anger. "Why did you bring me here?" she asked.

"What do you mean? I thought you wanted something new, something exciting. I guess this is all technically old, but you can't argue that it isn't exciting." Luke's grin put Mary instantly at ease, but only a little. She had seen too much, too quickly. "Do you know where you come from, my dear? Have you studied your family?"

Mary shook her head. "I know I'm mostly Irish," she replied.

"Yes, on your maternal great-grandmother's side. She was all fire, that one..."

Before Mary could question what was said, a man in a long, dark cloak appeared next to Luke. "How goes the war, My Lord?" he asked in the driest voice Mary had ever heard. It reminded her of sand falling onto glass.

"Boring, mostly. There's simply no challenge, anymore," Luke replied.

The cloaked figure nodded, sagely.

"War?" Mary asked.

"Oh, it's just an exaggeration – an old bet, really. Nothing important." He turned to Mary, silently dismissing the cloaked figure, who backed away with a bow and a flourish, vanishing into the crowd. "Are you hungry?"

"I don't know... I guess."

Luke turned to Gregory and waved him over. "Food for the lady," he said. Gregory nodded, and went into the back room from which he had originally emerged.

"But I didn't order anything," Mary protested.

"That doesn't matter, he knows what you want."

Mary thought for a moment. "Why didn't he know what I wanted to drink, then?" she smiled at Luke, who grinned wolfishly back.

"Because I wouldn't let him," he replied.

"He's not going to come back with the souls of the unborn on a gilded platter or something, is he?" Mary chuckled.

Luke turned to her. "Why?" he asked, "Is that what you wanted?" His eyes contained all the seriousness of a cataclysm.

"I...uh..."

And then he smiled, and everything was okay again.

The night passed pleasantly enough. Before long, it was getting late and Mary began to grow tired, though Luke showed no sign of slowing. On her way back from the restroom, where she had been receiving makeup tips from a haughty woman in the mirror, Mary spotted a rather handsome looking gentleman in the crowd.

He had the deepest eyes she had ever seen. She felt drawn to him, compelled to walk over and talk to him. She looked toward Luke, who was making small talk at the bar with creatures of various size and reality, then she smiled mischievously, and walked into the crowd.

The gentleman said nothing; he simply looked Mary in the eye, took her hand, and walked her out to the dance floor. Mary didn't resist – she didn't want to.

They began dancing a slow waltz, which Mary found herself knowing intricately. The waltz sped up, and they both kept pace. She laughed with pleasure. Then the music took a turn for the wild – a sharp, erratic jungle beat. Suddenly they were dancing strangely, more like sex than moving together in any noticeable rhythm. Mary loved it. The man kissed her neck and grabbed her ass, leading her around the room as she swooned back against his arms. She was incredibly and oddly close to orgasm, when suddenly it all stopped.

She opened her eyes, wondering when she had closed them, and looked into Luke's glaring face. "What exactly do you think you are doing?" he asked the man, still holding her by the waist. The man blanched.

"Lord, I...I didn't..." he stuttered.

"That's right, you didn't." Luke looked at the man with more hatred than Mary had ever seen. "What shall I do with you?" his voice was deadly calm. He pulled Mary away, who suddenly became aware that she needed to sit down, then smiled at the man, but there was no mirth in his eyes. "I know."

And he touched the man's shoulder. Before Mary's eyes, the man's stunning good looks withered – his nose became bulbous and covered in warts, his eyebrows merged into one, his skin broke out in boils, his brow sunk over one eye, his lips became limp and quivered spittle down his now nearly concaved chin. He was hideous. "There," Luke said, proudly.

Mary gaped in horror. "What did you do?"

"I punished him," Luke replied, plainly.

"But... I don't understand. Why? What is he?"

"An enemy, now. He was imprinting himself on you, and I can't have someone controlling one who is under my protection for the evening, now can I?"

"But..."

"It was the most fitting punishment I could think of on the spot, but if you have better ideas in mind...?"

Mary pulled away from him. "What are you?"

Luke simply laughed. "I think you know," he said, and smiled. He put his arm around her, and continued, "And I don't think you care." Then he kissed her, passionately, and he was right – she did know, and she no longer cared what he was, so long as she was his, forever.

And she was.

Not my Proudest Moment

One evening, my best friend and I went out to a local arcade. We were too young to drive, so we caught a ride from my brother. When we were ready to return home, we tried calling to get picked up, only to get a busy signal. We called several more times on the six mile walk home from various gas stations and stores, but with the same result. My brother had left the phone off the hook. It's not important to the story, but I thought you might like to know.

We were nearing the halfway point of our journey, on the sidewalk of a main artery of a street – a four lane speedway named Division. There was a taco place coming up, and, being hungry, we decided we'd stop and get some greasy, delicious, horrible-for-you tacos.

But on the sidewalk outside of the fast food restaurant, there was a little boy. I say little, but the term is relative. The boy was maybe ten years old, probably a little younger. He was curled up in the fetal position, bawling, on the sidewalk, in the dark. I noticed him as me and my friend approached.

Behind the crying child there were four other boys, (slightly older, maybe 12 or 13) some of them on bikes, some of them on foot. They were all looking at the boy with obvious amusement on their faces, as if they enjoyed the pain the boy was in.

I was instantly offended by them. I wanted to yell at them, to insult them, to challenge them or to scare them. As we approached, I wanted to kneel down and help the crying boy. I wanted to ask him what was wrong, what happened, why he was crying. I wanted to do something decent. I thought about doing all of these things, and several of them in combination, as we approached the boy and his sobs.

When we got to the boy, we paused for a moment – a very, very brief moment – then we both stepped over the crying figure and past the other boys, into the taco restaurant. We ordered our tacos. We sat down to eat. We ate, slowly, talking about various things, telling jokes, observing the attractive girls in the room as obviously as we could. When we left, the boys and the child were all gone. We continued on and eventually reached my house and, I believe, went to a party later.

I rationalized my actions back then. I thought that I didn't know the whole situation, and that the boy might have been a brother to one of the older kids. I thought that maybe he had fallen off his own bike, though I don't recall seeing one. I thought about those and a hundred other perfectly reasonable explanations that would ease my feelings of betrayal of a complete stranger, but somehow, I always knew I was wrong. I was wrong to leave him there – to simply step over someone in my path who was in tears and in need of help.

I learned something from all of this, eventually. It turns out, thinking about doing something decent doesn't count for shit.

The High Cost of Living

At the end of his life, just prior to letting go and traveling to the undiscovered country, Virgil thought about what it was that he would miss most about living. Kissing, maybe? Or sunshine? A cool breeze on a hot day? Sex?

He laid back in his antiseptic-white hospital bed and struggled to get comfortable. Death should have come for him by now. Hell, it should have come for him years ago. It had so very many chances. He recalled the time he caught a terrible flu only a few years back. After a week of pain and misery, of living in his own sweat and puking up nothing but bile because he dared not eat, he found that he was still alive. He wasn't sure, at the time, if he was grateful for that or not. But here, so close to the end, he decided that a few extra years were exactly what he had needed to get his affairs in order.

On a more logical (or possibly morose) day, he had even ordered his own casket and burial plot. Somebody had to do it, after all, and he had no remaining children to do it for him. The war had seen to that.

That damn war – ten years gone and they're still debating over what it was about. At the time, it made so much sense, but after... nothing seemed like it could be worth such a price.

A nurse came in and checked the machines nearby. She shook her head a little, then left without saying a word. Virgil smiled. He'd worked very hard to get the staff here to hate him enough to leave him alone. No fake smiles, no inflated conversation, and this way, when he dies, nobody will be anything but thankful. He briefly wondered if anyone had figured out his scheme, then decided it didn't really matter if they had.

His thoughts wandered back to the times he should have died. He'd nearly drowned in the ocean, caught in an undertow and breathing salt water for a short time, he'd survived being shot in an attempted mugging, two car crashes, one heart bypass surgery, allergic reaction to shellfish... he could have died in the womb, even. The doctors were all amazed that he came out the chute healthy and screaming.

Then he recalled his own children. His son was a jaundiced baby, but recovered quickly, and had twenty-four glorious years. His daughter, always the kind one, went to the war for nursing duties, "to help people" she had said. She never came back. He wiped away the tear that was trailing its way down his cheek. *It's been quite the trip*, he thought.

He didn't see the man sitting next to him enter. In fact, he only noticed him when he took the newspaper he was reading and snapped it out to fold it away.

"It's impossible to get accurate news these days," the man tch'd, then looked up. "You would be Virgil?"

Virgil nodded. "Who the fuck are you?"

The stranger smiled. "I'm your Broker."

"My broker? Well, fuck-off, I have all of my affairs in order."

"Oh?" the stranger kept smiling.

"Yeah. I'm letting my nephew decide what to do with all of what's left. See? Handled."

The Broker laughed. "I think your nephew would be out of his depth in this matter."

"Impossible. He's a smart kid – passed the board exam last year. He can handle it," Virgil replied smugly and with just a hint of pride.

"I see." The Broker stroked his chin. "Perhaps he could handle it, at that. But just the same, I think I had better explain things to you."

"Well hurry it up, can't you see I'm dying?"

The man laughed. "No, Virgil, you're dead." The words created a hollow silence all their own.

"What are you talking about? I'm talking to you, ain't I?"

"Yes." The Broker straightened his tie. It had a stick figure man carrying a briefcase on the bottom that was saying *it's better than shoveling shit*. "None the less, you are dead, and I am here to facilitate your transition and set your remaining property to its final location."

"You're full of it," Virgil growled, but didn't seem to believe the words himself.

The Broker sighed. "Your chest doesn't hurt when you breathe anymore, does it?"

"Well, no." Virgil took a few breaths to make certain. "But that's just the pain killers doing their job."

The stranger calmly shook his head. "Your vision is no longer cloudy, your mind is active and imaginative, you've even grown younger, Virgil." He took up a small hand mirror from his briefcase and held it up for Virgil to look at, and it was true. He looked vital, and healthy, and irritated.

"What kind of bullshit is this?!" he shouted. He jumped up and cocked his arm back to flatten the Broker, but then hesitated. He looked down at his hands. "My skin... it's so... young," he breathed, "And my legs – I haven't gotten up that fast in years." He patted his chest and his biceps, felt around his mouth with his tongue, counting every tooth, he pulled up his hospital gown and held it with his chin to look down at his penis, then dropped the gown back into place, sat down, and smiled.

Quickly, far too quickly, the smile faded. "What's the use of being young again if I can't do anything with it? I mean, if I'm really dead–"

"You are."

"–then, it's just not fair." His lip began to quiver.

"You are young because is it important for this transaction that you know exactly what you are selling, and how valuable it is. This is best expressed if you aren't old and broken-down."

Virgil was quiet for a moment. He thought about the situation and everything that the Broker had said, and noticed that thinking really was easier to do; less chaotic, quicker. "Alright. So what exactly is it that I'm selling?" he said, finally.

The Broker stood up, holding out a large stack of crisp white paper. At the top was Virgil's name in gold lettering. Below that, the letters became too small to read. He took a breath, let it out, and stated simply: "Your life."

"What do you mean, 'my life'? It's mine!" Virgil squinted at the contract.

"You mean you want to live it all over again? How dull."

"Hey!"

"Oh, I see. First time through for you, isn't it?" The Broker looked him up and down. "Yes, should have seen it before. Of course, you can re-live the same life all over again, but there will be some memory problems. For example, you might remember some things before they actually happen."

"Hold it!" Virgil shouted. "What else is there? What other options do I have?"

"Well, you can stay dead, if you like. Take some time off, be a god someplace, but that's strictly for the megalomaniacs and people who keep ant farms. You could go to your choice of afterlife, good or bad." He leaned in and lowered his voice, "Between you and me, you'd be amazed how much fun being tortured for a few hundred years can be." He wiggled his eyebrows at Virgil and smiled.

"Next," Virgil groaned.

The Broker rolled his eyes. "Fine. Our most popular option is to sell your life to someone else. You sell the entire thing for someone else to live through, making their own choices with what they find, as you did."

Virgil thought for a moment. "Won't that mess up history? Changing one person's life like that?"

"No," the Broker scoffed, "of course not." The confusion on Virgil's face had seemed to make a home there. The Broker sighed. "Haven't you ever felt like you were the only real person on the planet, and that everyone else was simply part of your world, or your dream, or figments of your imagination? Well, that's because they were."

Virgil furrowed his eyebrows. "So... none of it was real? None of it mattered?"

"What are you talking about? Of course it was *real*."

"But... the war, the things I've seen, the people I loved..."

"All happened. The lives you create go on to be available to first-timers, like you were. The history of your life is recorded and kept with this Life to let the buyer know what can be expected. And, of course, you lived it. That counts for something."

Virgil straightened and lowered his voice. "My children died in that war," he said, sadly.

"Yes. Well, some lives are shorter than others. No refunds, I'm afraid." The Broker opened his briefcase again. "Have you made up your mind? Which option sounds the best?"

Virgil glanced around the office he suddenly found himself standing in. "What happened to the hospital?"

"Oh, we left there a long time ago. Depressing place to conduct business, anyway."

Virgil sat down in a comfortable wingback chair across the desk from the Broker. "So, what exactly am I, then? Now, I mean."

"You're an –" he looked down at the forms in front of him, "Aura. No, wait –western– you're a soul. At least, that's the best description available from the life you've lived."

Virgil nodded, then sat back and contemplated things for a moment. "Tell me honestly, Broker, is my life... valuable?"

"Honestly? As far as human lives go on earth, I've seen better." He glanced over the forms. "Children for only a short while, never married, no real friends to speak of... other than the near-death junkies and the misery lovers, you'd be lucky to sell this life for much of anything. You'd certainly have a hard time affording another." The Broker set the paperwork down and absentmindedly played with some weighted metal balls on strings hung in a line on his desk. Virgil watched the balls clack back and forth for a bit, wondering what to do.

Then he spoke up. "Can I make different choices? If I do it all again, I mean."

The Broker shrugged and moved his head from side to side as if mentally balancing scales. "Welllllll.... kind of. You see, you're still the same *You*, and very few people retain any information about any of this when they go back. The human brain is simply too linear to grasp it all comfortably. So, really, you'd likely just do the same thing all over again."

"Yes, but you said some bits of memory from my old life stick around, like a warning or something. Maybe it's enough."

"Enough for what?"

"...to not regret how lonely my life has been," Virgil replied. A tear welled up in his eye and rolled down his face.

The Broker sighed. "I get barely any commission at all for cases like you." He took a single sheet of paper from a pocket in his briefcase and slid it across the desk to Virgil. "Sign this."

Virgil grabbed the ballpoint pen that sat in an ornate holder on the desk, and glanced at the form. "I don't have to sign it in blood or anything?"

"No." The Broker looked confused and a little excited. "Why? Would you like to?"

Virgil shrugged, and signed a name that was familiar, and certainly was his own signature, but in no way resembled the name 'Virgil'. And he went back to his old life, born again to a group of surprised doctors, and grew up, and made changes, and died, and another broker got his case, but I must confess I don't know if things are turning out for the better or for the worse.

With all of life's ups and downs, I'm afraid I lost track of you a long time ago. I didn't want to, It just happened. And now you know why I'm writing this. You captivated me with your resolute stubbornness, your absolute unwillingness to have a poor life, your inability to let go of the only life you ever knew. Do you understand? You see, I just had to know – how are you doing, Virgil?

Twist of Fate

Please be patient. Your life is important to us. You will be returned to your usual existence as soon as possible.

The waiting room was immaculate – the kind of clean that you wish operating rooms and tattoo parlors would be, but never seem to achieve. Stainless steel gleamed from every door handle and bit of trim around the spotless glass windows. Sun shined through them onto a sterile white tile floor.

Through the window was a city of glowing gold and greenery. Forests rested atop buildings, synthetic land bridges between them had great fields and paths to direct foot traffic. It was a perfect day and, somehow, it seemed certain that it always would be.

Please answer the red courtesy telephone, a dull recording droned. The phone was answered.

"Ah, yes, hello," said a busy voice on the other end, "Good day. Sorry for the inconvenience. Now, we need to get you set straight." The sound of papers rustling could be heard through the phone speaker. "Okay. Born, good childhood, more or less decent parents, some law breaking in the early teens.... oh-" the decidedly male voice stopped short. The phone went dead, but was not hung up.

After what may have been minutes, or centuries, or just a lifetime, the voice came back. "Um... work with me on this, okay? There may be some confusion..."

And then Tom woke up. He was tired. It was his day off, so he knew he didn't have to be awake yet, but here he was. He turned over and buried himself in the sheets once again, but try as he might, he simply couldn't fall back to sleep. He growled into his pillow. Eventually, he persuaded himself to join the waking world, and got out of bed.

His roommate sat in the living room, watching a woodworking program on public broadcasting. "I had the strangest dream," Tom said, yawning.

"Can it wait? This guy is awesome. He does all of his projects without power tools. It's amazing," Dave, his roommate, said without looking away from the television.

140

Tom shrugged for his own benefit, and went into the kitchen to pour himself some cereal. The cartoon character on the box made him wonder if he was still a part of the target audience for this particular brand, but he decided he didn't really care, and did the crossword and maze on the back of the box instead.

There was a knock on the door. Tom got up and answered it. A man in a cleaned and pressed suit stood there, looking hopeful. "Have you accepted our lord and savior into your life?" the man asked.

"No," Tom replied, "Tried once. We argued a lot."

"I see. Well, it's never too late," the man continued, "Perhaps I can leave some literature with you and you can read it at your leisure." His tone was grating, overly helpful, like a teacher's pet ratting on his classmates.

"Nope, I'm afraid I'm illiterate," Tom said, calmly staring the visitor in the eye.

The man was undeterred. "Perhaps there is someone else in the household I could speak to?"

"No, I live alone," Tom replied, then closed the door as the man attempted to continue his pre-recorded speech. Tom moseyed back to the dining room table, but stopped to wonder why this woodworking show was on. He hated shows like that, they always made him feel like he couldn't do anything interesting or amazing. He turned off the television and went back to his cereal to continue the crossword.

After his breakfast, he spent some on a website putting up an advertisement for a roommate. The extra room in the apartment stood empty and needed filling soon if he was to be able to afford the rent.

That's not it yet.
I'm doing it. Don't tell me what to do.

Samantha walked out of the bedroom in her form fitting bra and underwear. She stretched luxuriously, like a waking cat, one section of body at a time. Then, she walked over to Tom and threw her arms around his shoulders.

"Good morning," she said, kissing his neck in that particular spot that he liked.

"Sleep well?" Tom replied as best he could.

"Yeah, but for some reason I really want to go back to bed," Samantha teased, then bit him playfully.

Tom turned around and tickled her sides. She shrieked and jumped back, then leapt at him. At some point that neither of them could identify, their playful fighting and wrestling on the floor turned into passionate sex. Neither of them minded.

Why did you stop? That was getting good.
My pen ran out of ink. Besides, it wasn't going right.
Maybe if you—
No. This is bound to work.

Tom awoke to his alarm playing some asinine pop song about love. He groaned and slammed his fist into the alarm clock, stopping the mindless drivel. He got up, showered, brushed his teeth, and got dressed in his work uniform without thinking. He included a button exclaiming 'Ask me about our summer deals!' Whenever someone actually asked, he simply stared at them, blankly, until they went away.

The blowout with Samantha last night had been painful, and prolonged, but a long time coming. He found himself sitting on the edge of his bed, contemplating calling in and pretending to be sick, but decided against it. He needed the money, even though it would never be enough to pay for this apartment by the end of the month. His eyes fell upon the pistol case which was peeking out of the closet like a coquettish girl doing a fan-dance, but he decided against that, too.

> *That's not right.*
> *I told you to let me do it.*
> *Shut up. I know what I'm doing.*

Work was a few miles away, across a massive bridge that passed over some old train tracks, and connected a steep hillside with the downtown district. He arrived at his job – a rundown coffee shack that served second rate swill to the local laborers and students from a nearby college who didn't know any better. He straightened the button on his shirt that read 'Have a caffeinated day!' and had a smiling cartoon-faced sun with coffee cups for eyes. He shuffled into the shack.

He hung up his coat.

He folded his coat over his arm.

He shivered in the morning chill because he had absentmindedly forgotten his coat at home that morning.

This isn't working.
Don't you think I know that?
What are you going to do?
This.

Tom stood in an amazingly bright room. His head was killing him, his mind tried to compensate for memories inexplicably taking place at the same moment as others in different locations, thousands of near identical memories with only minor discrepancies. It did this, chiefly, by panicking. Tom clutched his skull and fell to his knees in agony.

"Thomas Ringwall?" a kind voice asked.

Suddenly the pain was gone. It was as if his mind had taken into account all that was happening to it, and then sat back to see what would happen, because it sure as hell wasn't going to clean up this mess.

"Thomas?" the same voice prodded, "Are you alright?"

Tom stood up, and looked into the face of a young man with dark brown hair, a child with a gap-toothed smile, and an old, bald man with a long beard and a wart on his cheek that had several dark hairs growing from it. The odd thing was, they were all the same person. Tom's mind gave up.

144

"I know the process can be painful," the old man said, fading away and morphing into the middle aged one, who continued, "Can I get you anything?"

"Nothing, thanks," Tom said, his brow furrowed. "Who're you?"

"Oh, I hardly think that matters," the child piped.

"Tell him! I want to see his face!" shouted a high pitched voice from somewhere nearby.

"It isn't conducive to our goals." The man was just an outline of light now, his voice a long remembered echo, but he was quickly growing back into a solid person once more.

"Where am I?" Tom pressed on.

"I'm afraid that's a little difficult to explain. You're nowhere, technically. At least, nowhere you could point to on a map."

"Yeah! No 'You Are Here' signs like in the malls!" the voice shouted once again. Tom looked around the room for the source.

"Who is that?" he asked.

"Oh, he's um... how do I put this?" The old man stroked his grey beard, which folded into baby fat. "He's Curiosity," the child said, smiling.

Somehow, that made perfect sense to Tom. "Why can't I see him?"

"What would you expect Curiosity to look like?" the middle aged man asked.

"I dunno. A lot of things, I guess."

The man smiled. "Exactly."

"So, where is he?"

"Everywhere," the middle aged man said as Tom looked around the room in vain, then continued, "He's very good at his job."

"Tell him what you are!" Curiosity shouted. Tom wondered why he always shouted.

"Fine," the old man barked, then sighed, "I'm Fate."

"Fate?" Tom looked him over, "Like, *The* Fate? Of everything?"

"Oh, no, not at all. Only a few thousand souls," Fate looked down, bashfully, "I'm just doing my share."

Tom nodded. "So, not that I'm not having a great time, but what the hell am I doing here?"

"That's easy: I need your help," Fate said, simply.

"Wait, *Fate* needs my help? Isn't it your job to, I dunno, control what's going to happen?"

"Well, yes, of course. Only... no, not this time." He paced around Tom for a moment. "You see," continued the old man, in between bouts of being an infant, a young executive, and not there at all, "sometimes, mistakes are made."

"Hold on a sec, you were in my dream!" Tom realized, suddenly.

"There was no dream. That was just a review, a reboot if you like."

"I remember your voice. You got off that phone pretty damn quick." Tom was indignant, an inch away from rage.

"I was just trying to help." The old man looked down, sadly. "I can move things around, you see. I

146

thought that if I changed enough, I could avoid a darker path."

"He's new," said Curiosity with a snicker from the mouth of a passing cat.

"I gave you different choices to make, millions of them, billions really, and billions within those billions, but none of them worked out quite right," Fate's voice was low, distant.

"So, you fucked with my life and messed up the universe, right?" Tom said, with just a hint of pride.

"What? No, of course not. You see, usually you can just move choices around. As long as events are set in motion somehow, it doesn't matter who did the initial action. I mean, really, how important is one person when their actions are replaced by someone else who's doing the same thing? But, sometimes, there's a snag."

"Tell him about Joan!" cried a raven who flew through the room from a sudden storm outside, and back out into the storm once more. Tom wondered where it went, and where it came from.

"I'm handling this!" Fate shouted after it. "So, as I was saying-"

"I'm important," Tom blurted out, and smiled. "What, do I save the world or something?"

"No," Fate looked him in the eye, more solid than he'd been since Tom's arrival, "You're supposed to be dead."

The words landed heavily on Tom's shoulders. Even the ever-intrusive Curiosity was silent. "What do you mean? I can't die," Tom laughed half-heartedly, "I

147

mean, you've spent all this time trying to prevent that, right? That was the 'darker path' you were talking about, wasn't it? How can I be of any help if I'm dead?"

"I know it doesn't seem to make much sense, but it's important. You have to die. Every single possible life you might lead must end, and they must end while you are young."

Tom turned away from the changing face of Fate and stood, conflicted, repeatedly balling his hands into fists and releasing them. He turned back. "No," he said.

Tom left the coffee shack after his shift. He drove towards home over the same tall bridge, and didn't drive off the edge. He didn't turn into oncoming traffic. When he got home, he didn't look longingly at the pistol in its case, and he didn't pick up a razor to split his flesh while he was drinking. In fact, he didn't even drink.

"You can't just refuse," the old man said. Tom crashed back to the too-clean room. "You have to die, Thomas."

"You don't know what you're talking about!" Tom screamed, "What good is my dying? What's the point?!"

Fate took a deep breath, and let it out. He nodded slightly, coming to a decision. "You remember Samantha?" he asked in the high tones of a child.

"No," Tom replied, then, "Yes, of course. We were together for years. Or, we are together... uh..."

Fate interrupted him by placing a hand, gently, on his shoulder. "Don't stress yourself," he said. He leaned to one side and the other, mentally weighing options. Tom got the impression that he was weighing the differences in the lifetime of a universe, in billions of years of history, changed by the words he was about to say. "Samantha is the important one," he said, finally, "and it's your death that inspires her to do great things. Even in the timelines where she only knows you in passing, you have a profound effect on her. As lovers, or ex-lovers, she feels your death personally. We've tried others, millions of others, but they didn't have the same effect. There's something about you, Thomas, something we can't identify. You're the catalyst for her greatness." He looked at Tom, hopefully, sadly.

"I don't want..." Tom faltered.

"Would you like him to change it so you do?" Curiosity butted in.

Fate shook his head. "It's too late for that. I changed too much. That's why I brought you here. I thought if I could tell you, personally, what had happened... I'm afraid you'll never want to die, Tom, but you have to, regardless."

"And what happens if I refuse?" Tom asked.

"I told you, you don't have that luxury."

"Of course I do. Why else would you drag me here?" Fate was quiet, so Tom continued. "Now tell me, what happens if I just *don't* die?"

Fate hesitated. He glanced sidelong at Curiosity, who shrugged the shoulders of a rat in an *"it wasn't me"* kind of way. Finally, he spoke. "If you live, Samantha will never reach her potential, not really. Sometimes she'll think she's happy, sometimes she'll be overtly miserable, but always she will die, not only unrealized, but unwilling and unable to reach for her goals. She'll be a wasted life, Thomas," the infant's high tone finished.

Tom looked at Fate for a long moment. He shook his head in disbelief. "This is..." he shook his head once again, "Why did you have to fuck with everything? Why couldn't you just let me die?!"

"I took pity on you, Tom. I thought... I thought you deserved better, that you didn't have to die." He lowered his head. "I'm sorry."

Tom raised his fist to hit the man, the child, everything that made up Fate, but hesitated. He struggled with the thought for a while, but let it fall in the end. Tears began to form in his eyes. "I can't," he said.

"You must."

Worlds formed and crumbled in the time that Tom stood there, debating, processing what he's been told. Eventually, shyly, he asked, "Does it hurt?"

"I don't know," Fate replied. His shape changed less, now. His movements slowed. "I hope not." Tom nodded in understanding. "Are you ready?"

"No," Tom replied, "But let's do it anyway."

Tom absentmindedly walked into the street while heading home from school. He was just a boy – he wasn't looking for passing cars. A young girl read about it. She found it so sad, so pointless, that she endeavored to never let herself be left to oblivion, never to be useless.

Tom had broken up with Samantha the night before. He sat on his bed in an apartment that he would soon lose, before work. His eyes fell upon the pistol lying in its case in the closet. He made up his mind. Samantha was shattered, wracked with guilt, and pity, and anger at what Tom had done. It was selfish, she decided eventually, and resolved not to let him win. She was going to do something with her life, something important.

It was a freak accident, they said. Tom somehow lost control of his car, and it careened off of the bridge onto the railroad tracks below. His girlfriend, Samantha, was horrified. She spent months just getting herself back together again. Finally, she decided she would dedicate herself to living enough for the both of them, and she did.

Samantha was awoken one night by a strange noise. In her sleep-blurred vision, she saw Tom standing in the middle of the floor. She didn't notice the gun in his hand. Later, she told her closest friends that the oddest part of the whole tragedy was that she could have sworn Tom had whispered, "I don't want to die," just before he pulled the trigger.

And he died.
And he died.
And he died.

The Wrath of Thalia

Charles sat in his booth in the audio effects department, going through the program his studio had just completed. His job was to add the laughter and other background noises at appropriate volumes and constancy for the joke being told or the situation the character had gotten himself into. He'd only been at this job for a couple of months, more or less doing the same thing every day, and was already thoroughly bored. On the screen in front of him, the protagonist of the series (a carefree-haphazard type that was always so damn clever) made a slight joke. Charles added a *medium density laughter*. The sassy ex-girlfriend made a hurtful retort. Charles turned up the laughter intensity and added some '*Woo*'s' for good measure.

The door burst open behind him, and Charles calmly stopped the playback. He swiveled his squeaky chair around for the inevitable, and wasn't disappointed. The head of the after effects department in the studio stood before him, fuming. "You missed an entire joke last week!" the man shouted, skipping all pleasantries.

"I didn't miss it," Charles replied, "The joke just worked better without the laugh track." He shrugged.

The man shook his head which sent the fat swaying about his chins. His hair-piece moved just a little bit after he did, like it was ashamed to be following his lead. He gripped the lapels of his expensive suit jacket and said, "Charles, you just don't get it. If you don't add the laugh track, how will people know what's funny?"

Charles debated explaining the concept of humor to his boss, but for the sake of his job, he held his tongue. "I see what you mean," he said, haltingly. He hated himself for it immediately.

"Well, no more playing around with the way things work, alright? Now, back to it. I want this episode done by Friday." And with that, the suit left the room. His hair piece followed.

Charles counted to thirty, took a deep breath, let it out slowly... then threw his empty coffee mug at the closed door as hard as he could. It shattered. One sharp edged piece spun like a top on the floor for several seconds before falling. He imagined adding-in the *awkward cough* track. Unable to work, and rather than sitting around wasting the day, he declared to his immediate manager that he wasn't feeling well and went home early.

Just as he got out of the studio door, it started to downpour. He ran to his car and jumped in as quickly as he could. Sopping wet and soaked through his thin jacket, he looked up at the sky through his windshield just in time to see the rain stop. *Cue the mild chuckles,* he thought. He sighed and drove home under a sunny sky.

The next morning, he went into work and sat down in his usual spot to begin the playback. His coworker, Jack, looked over at him. "So, you having the dreams yet?" he asked, grinning. Charles shook his head. "Give it time," Jack continued, "it'll happen."

Jack was sure that everyone who worked this job long enough developed laugh tracks to their sleep, but Charles still wasn't convinced. On the playback, the main character made an awful pun. Charles added a crowd-wide groan and a couple boos, just for kicks and a little bit of revenge. Jack, ever the long-time bored professional, looked over at Charles again but kept working, more out of habit than actual effort. "Do you know where most of these things come from?" he asked.

Charles paused his playback. "The laugh tracks? No, not really."

"Some dude in the 40's or 50's recorded 'em – to replace the live audience feel in a non-live show, you know?" He smiled.

154

Charles nodded. "Wait, all of these can't be that old."

"Well, some of 'em have been updated, like the ones where some dude coughs or clears his throat, some of those are new. For realism, I guess. But most studios figure 'what the hell, we bought 'em years ago, we might as well use 'em.' Free is a great price for anything." Jack laughed and Charles cringed. After so many years working here, Jack's laughter sounded eerily like the people on the laugh track.

The rest of the shift was quieter than usual.

Jack had left a while ago. Charles sat alone in the dimly lit booth finishing his work before the coming deadline tomorrow morning. Finally, he came to the last scene: a big romantic kiss between the two most unlikely, and thus destined to fall in love, characters. He played them out with cheers and applause and catcalls and began to wonder how Jack had been at this job for so long.

He turned off the equipment and yawned. He grabbed his coat and walked out the door.

A spotlight flooded his vision with blinding white light. At first, all he knew was the light and how bright it was, but then the applause started – roaring applause, hundreds of people, clapping. His vision adjusted and he found himself walking across a brilliantly colored stage, all pastels and sparkles, then he heard an announcer. "Let's meet tonight's contestant! Ladies and gentlemen, Charles Douglass!"

The crowd redoubled their efforts, but try as he might, Charles couldn't see them – he just heard and felt their cheers. A man dressed in an evening suit came out and shook his hand, then doffed his bowler to him, showing a bare head with two small horns protruding at the front. The man quickly replaced his hat.

"Welcome to the show, Charles, and congratulations!" the man waited for the clapping to die down once more. "Tell me, have you seen the show at home before? Do you know the rules?"

Charles fidgeted with the coat in his hands and stuttered, "Uh...no, I... uh–"

"No? Never?" the man sounded hurt, but then gave a full-toothed grin, and happily continued, "Well then, let's go over the rules before we begin." The man, who seemed to be the host, tilted his hat forward a little so it came down to just above his eyes. "First off, you'll be playing against our audience. It's their job not to react, at all, to anything that you do, and it's your job to get a reaction from them. Now, for a third place prize, you've gotta make 'em angry, and then run out of town before they lynch you." He leered in the direction of the audience and the audience laughed. "For a second place prize, you've gotta make 'em cry. And for the grand prize, you've got to–!" he pointed at the audience, and as one voice they chanted:

"MAKE. US. LAUGH!" and the applause erupted, bombarding Charles with such strength that he fell to his knees and clapped his hands over his ears. After a moment, the earth shattering noise subsided. The host sidled over and touched Charles' shoulder.

"Get up!" he hissed, keeping the microphone away from his mouth. Charles stood up, unsteadily. He could feel the stare of the crowd and the cameras upon his dumbfounded face. "Well, you're on your way to making them incredibly bored," The host said into the mic. The audience laughed. "So, are you ready? Let's begin."

The stage went black, leaving only a single spotlight focused on Charles. After a moment, there was the sound of a cricket gently screeching somewhere off stage. "Um..." Charles started. Sweat broke out on his forehead. The silence pressed heavily upon him, and for a moment he thought he knew what Giles Corey must have felt in the end.

Every few thousand years, a second passed. He cleared his throat, found out that his tongue was indeed still attached to his mouth somewhere, organized his thoughts, cleared his throat once more, and said, "*Shit*," quietly.

It started with a single guffaw, somewhere up front. It could have been a cough, really, but the second giggle, stifled near the back, that one was definitely real. And then there was another, a chuckle, somewhere in the center of the crowd, and another – they were beginning to blend together, becoming a quiet amalgamation of amusement. It was absurd, but people were laughing – more at themselves than at Charles, but they were still laughing. Charles smiled.

Suddenly, the spotlight went out and all sound ceased. A chill breeze blew across Charles' skin. "Did... did I win?" he asked the darkness.

His voice echoed back to him, "Win? Did...I Did...Win?" and then a harsh whisper, "Yes." The stage lights came on once again. The host was standing next to him, carefully inspecting his bowler hat. "Yes, you won," he said dryly. "It's not a great accomplishment. It's not like you could have lost."

"What do you mean?"

"Have you looked out at the audience, yet? I mean, really looked at them?"

"What do you–?"

"Look at them, Charles," The host said, kindly, removing a speck of dust from his hat.

And Charles looked.

"But they're..." he breathed.

"Yes." The host replaced his hat. "They always were."

"Then how did they–?" Charles began, but a chorus of cheers and applause cut him off. He looked at the host, and the noise of the crowd stopped.

"You see?" The host began to walk away, then paused. He turned back to Charles and said, "But you must wonder, if they had their choice, would they still have laughed?" He smiled.

"Good morning ladies and gents, it's a balmy 93 degrees outside today, and traffic is backed up all the way to the tunnel. Now here's the latest hit from –"

Charles slammed his fist down on the alarm clock, killing the all-too-cheery DJ's voice. He got out of bed and yawned. The world looked unbelievably normal now – peaceful.

He did his usual morning routine and went to work. Jack was already sitting in his chair and waved at him as he sat down, then paused. He took off his headset, but didn't pause the playback. Charles could hear it from where he sat. "You had the dream, didn't you?" Jack smiled.

"I had *a* dream, yes."

"Told you you'd have it sooner or later."

A thought occurred to Charles. "Hey, the people that recorded the original laugh tracks back in the day, they'd mostly be dead by now, wouldn't they?"

"I dunno, I guess so. Why?"

A wave of humor washed over Charles, and he smiled. He was about to laugh, but the dead in Jack's headset did it for him, and he wondered for the first time if they were laughing at the same thing.

An Interview for the Morning Edition

-Begin Transcript-

Interviewer: Thank you for taking time out of your busy schedule to meet with us today.

Lucifer: Not at all. I always have time for my friends.

Interviewer: I'm flattered, sir. So, to begin, many of my subscribers thought you would be the one to ask this question: Where has God been?

160

Lucifer: He is where He has always been.

Interviewer: But has something happened? Things around here haven't been going well for quite some time.

Lucifer: (laughs) Why do people always assume that their era is worse than any other?

Interviewer: Well, I'm sure people are confident He is doing His job, but many are having trouble seeing His hand in the world these days.

Lucifer: (nods) It's understandable. Humans have always been a curious lot, and it's always getting them into trouble. It's the reason I like you so much. God has been... preoccupied.

Interviewer: Can you elaborate?

Lucifer: (smiles) Of course I can.

Interviewer: Will you?

Lucifer: No. Suffice it to say that He is no longer paying much attention to humanity.

Interviewer: I see. (pause) So, Lucifer, – can I call you Lucifer?

Lucifer: If it helps.

Interviewer: But, that is your name, isn't it?

Lucifer: I have many names, in many places, at many times. None of them are my own, but Lucifer has a nice biblical ring to it.

Interviewer: Alright. So, Lucifer, a lot of people have been wondering just how much of the world is your fault.

Lucifer: Excuse me?

Interviewer: Well, I mean, how many of the world's problems are your doing?

Lucifer: None.

Interviewer: Honestly?

Lucifer: Never. (laughs) No, really, my interfering with your world is infinitesimal, though I do get blamed for a great deal of it.

Interviewer: Then who is to blame?

Lucifer: *You* ask *me* that? It's amazing how your kind can be arrogant and stupid in equal measure and still control

162

the fate of an entire planet. Who do you think causes the lion's share of problems in your world?

Interviewer: I don't know.

Lucifer: Yes, you do.

Interviewer: I do?

Lucifer: Who burnt down your house when you were a child?

Interviewer: I don't know what tha–

Lucifer: Humor me.

Interviewer: That fire was caused by an electrical problem, if I recall.

Lucifer: Your sister died in that blaze, didn't she?

Interviewer: (silence)

Lucifer: So, a bit of faulty wiring killed your baby sister and burnt down your childhood home. It could have been anybody, but it just happened to be your house: an act of God, is that it?

Interviewer: It wasn't the wiring. They found a fuse that... that...

Lucifer: And if they hadn't found that fuse? If they had dug a little deeper? What would have been the cause of that inferno if they had ever suspected a small child that liked playing with fire?

Interviewer: I was only eight years old...

Lucifer: And had a fascination with flame: the color, the warmth, the power.

Interviewer: Idle hands are the devil's playthings.

Lucifer: (laughs) What would I want with idle hands when *active* ones are available, and so much more willing?

Interviewer: You caused me to pick up those matches.

Lucifer: Why would I do that? Your sister was due to be one of the most successful suicide cult leaders the world will ever see. No, I wanted her to live.

Interviewer: So I stopped that from happening when I– when the house burnt down.

Lucifer: It's possible, but in the grand mysteries and chaos of the universe, there could be something else afoot, or I may be lying. Maybe your sister would have saved millions of lives, somehow. Or maybe, just maybe, she wasn't worth my attention whatsoever.

Interviewer: You're confusing me.

Lucifer: (laughs) I know.

Interviewer: I hate you.

Lucifer: Is that any way to talk to a friend? But, to answer your question: people cause people's problems. And the fact is, they always have.

Interviewer: Well, you would say that.

Lucifer: (laughs) Yes, I would, wouldn't I?

-Transcript Ends-

A Letter to a Friend

When we were young, we would play in the fields behind my house. The grass and wild wheat would be as tall as we were, and we'd play hide-and-seek. I remember thinking I was clever, because I would leap into the field instead of running, making my trail harder to follow, but you always found me.

In the spring, we would chase after butterflies and pretend we could fly along with them, and in the evening, we would stand very still, and wait for them to get tired. They would land on us, do you remember? You got so scared and kept asking how such a beautiful creature could have such a terrifying face. I never let you live it down.

When we were older, and the other boys would pick on us, we would always fight back together. It was always the two of us. You were my best friend and my confidant. Can you imagine my surprise when they told me you didn't exist?

You were there, remember? The doctor said I was making you up – that you were all in my head. How could I have taken on all those other boys, then? Did I play hide and seek by myself? Am I really that crazy? I know you said they were lying, but I wasn't sure. I had to find out, you know? Do you understand?

The day I started taking the pills from the doctor, you told me not to. You were worried about what it could do to me; to us. It turns out, you were right to be worried.

First you got sick, and you couldn't get out of bed in the morning. That didn't stop us though, you had been sick before, but I hadn't realized up until then that it had always been when I was sick, too. We played cards and board games all day.

Soon, you were able to get out of bed, but you were angry with me. You were so easy to offend, then. I never did figure out why. Did you know what was happening to you? Did you blame me?

I remember the last day. I got out of bed in the morning, but I couldn't find you anywhere. I searched the entire house. I even asked my mom if she had seen you, but she just shook her head, sadly. I was alone all day. I got so worried about you that I didn't take my pills, and that night, when I was just dozing off to sleep, I heard you. You were coughing on the floor. I rushed to your side, asked you what happened, why you were so sick, what I could do, but you only smiled at me.

You kept saying you were cold, in the end. I cuddled up next to you, rubbed your shoulders, your arms, tried to warm you up, but you only got colder. Finally, I went to get my electric blanket from the bed, and when I turned around you were gone – only the cold floor looked back at me. I cried all night, and for the first time in my life, I didn't have you there to comfort me.

Months have passed since that night. Now, when the other boys pick on me, I don't always have the courage to fight back, but sometimes I remember you, and fight twice as hard. Yesterday, I went into the field behind my house and brought a shovel. I dug you a proper grave and buried a box to represent you. I even found a big rock for a headstone. In the evening, the butterflies came and rested on your grave mound, and, for once, you weren't afraid of their faces.

I held still for hours, but the butterflies won't come back to me anymore.

Acknowledgments

I would first like to thank you, yes *you*, the reader. Literature has very little point if people aren't reading it, and look at you. You're actually reading the acknowledgements. Who does that? Frankly, I'm impressed. Carry on, you magnificent creature. You have made my day.

Secondly, and only slightly less awesome than you (you're still here?) I would like to thank my family. My father doesn't read much outside of the funnies, but he was always there to listen to my readings and ranting about characters that wouldn't do what I wanted them to.

My sisters and brothers were supportive in every way possible, from going to my readings to financial support to get the book printed, as was my mother. I couldn't ask for a better family.

I hope that everyone, at some point in their lives, has a teacher who still gives a damn. Someone who still wants the best for their students and who still teaches with a passion that gets other people excited about what they're learning. For me, that teacher was Kasey Church. She cares about her students, in and out of class, and would make time for anyone having trouble. Without her help, I'm not sure I would have channeled my emotions into literature. I very nearly dedicated this book to her.

Leaving out my friends would be a grand oversight. I was lucky enough to have several talented people reviewing my work: Grant Burgess, Tiffani Graves, Leah Rivendell, Krista Guignard, Terry Greenwood, Jenny McAllister, Elizabeth Maulding, Amanda Gray, Dax Imber, Laci Lardin, Debbie Macey, and many others were all instrumental in helping to see this book come to fruition. When I needed someone to bounce strange ideas off of, you were there. You kept me company when I needed it, and gave me space when I wanted it. This would not be the same book without each and every one of you.

On the technical side of things, Elizabeth Maulding graciously allowed me to use her artwork for the paperback cover. If you'd be interested in getting to see more of her work or contacting her for commissioned work, feel free to send me an email and I'll put you in touch with her.

Benjamin Reed, photographer of BenReedStudios.com is responsible for the fantastic author picture on the reverse of the paperback. He does amazing work and is a pleasure to work with.

Several variant covers were created by various Portland artists and distributed to those who helped in the fundraiser to get this book printed, and though you may not be holding one of the variant books, I believe credit is due to those who supplied the absolutely stunning work:

-Lannie Alejandro Appel of AlejandroAppel.com created many of the digital artwork covers you may find floating around. He really is incredibly talented with a sharp wit.

-Laura Hippensteel of laurahippensteel.weebly.com created two covers as well, gorgeous pieces of art hand-drawn and inspired by the stories she read.

-Shelly Deangio, the talented licensed inksmith of Shell Shock Tattoos, also did a cover based on one of the stories.

-Leah Rivendell, an all-around scamp and fantastic human being. A dear friend, and lover of all living things. She's as close to a druid as I've known.

-Emilie Lemons was gracious and kind enough to supply me with a cover image for one of the variant covers. She is a very talented person in many respects. As proof, the cover she gave me she completed in under an

hour. It really is impressive. You can contact her at
www.facebook.com/sproutingcreations.emlem

Each of these people took time out of their lives to read my work, to become invested, and to donate their skill and artwork to making the outside of this book look as amazing as they possibly could. They shared their vision, and their passion, and I could not possibly ask for a better gift than that.

Lastly, I would like to thank people who work in coffee shops, any coffee shops. Even if it's just a diner that happens to sling very bad, very old, very burnt coffee, I want to thank you. Because of you and your ilk, I was able to maintain a level of sleep-deprived delusion that allowed me to connect with the abstract parts of my mind – with the dreams and the muses and the demons that make up the creatures in these stories and inspired these and many more.

~Sean Walter
April, 2014

172

Here's a section from one of Sean
Walter's upcoming books, *Moribund*

"People don't know how much of the system breaks down when just one or two parts stop working. The children of tomorrow will have to fend for themselves. They won't know how to purify their water, if they can find it. They won't know how to hunt or grow their food, if the soil is clean enough. They won't be able to power their cities, assuming civilization survives. In such a world, morals will be a laughable and quaint memory."

~*The Word of the People*

Year: 2076

World population: unknown

Early-fall, before high noon.

She sees him there, walking just a few dozen yards below her. He's very talented at moving, but the fresh kill on his back is a hindrance to his usually swift and silent movements. She supposes that he must have been out here a long time, away from the settlements and the rebuilding of "society."

But not long enough. If he'd been out here just a little while longer, he would have known not to bring his food through this area. He would have known not to carry it along in a valley where he can be easy prey for anyone watching. He would have known that the small designs scorched into many of the trees around this place marked this as her territory – only fools can't read such plain markings, and only fools don't leave tribute to the owner of the territory as they cross it.

She watches him wander along the easiest trail, and imagines that he is thanking whatever gods he believes in that he has found such a furnished path for him to carry his burden. *But to where does he carry it?* she thinks. She pictures him carrying it back to his family and being the conquering hero, bringing food to his loved ones. He's a decent looking man, she decides. Dark blond hair, broad shoulders, a good height, not too old – he even has a pretty face. She briefly entertains the notion of keeping him for sex and company, but quickly dismisses the idea as folly. Such a man would be a nuisance to train to live this far from the settlements, even if he could get past his aversion to her. *No...* she thinks, *the winter is coming, and I'm low enough on food as it is.*

She has been following him for a mile now, creeping along the dense underbrush, picking every step and weighing herself out slowly to keep from breaking an unseen twig or fumbling into one of her own man-traps. She knows what those in the settlements say about her. She's heard it many times from people that she's confronted – their last defiant insult before death.

"*Demon.*"

"*Soul-less.*"

She's earned these titles in every way. She's killed men, women, and occasionally children. She's rent flesh from bone, eaten it cooked and raw, and used their skins for boots and gloves and a hundred other things that

175

leather is useful for. "When I was young, most people didn't know how to do these things." her mother used to tell her, "But then they didn't have to, either."

The man pauses in the valley, laying down the slain animal and sitting below a small tree near the path. She takes this opportunity to go further down along the trail, remaining hidden from her prey as she does so. She had made the path deliberately during the wet spring months, reasoning that turning over the soaked soil would be heavier work, but getting the spade into the earth would be easier, and she was right. Delighting in the work at the time, she had thought of the catch to come in the next months just as any human laying a trap for any animal ever had.

She readies her rifle as she approaches her favorite vantage point. The point is simply a concrete ledge above a steep hill, roughly fifteen feet above the valley floor. The path here rounds an outcropping, once the corner of a building, before coming into view from her vantage point, forcing her prey to take a blind corner and allowing her to take them down without a fight. It's for this very reason that she chose this place as her kill zone.

It's another ten minutes before she can hear footsteps coming along the trail. She lays down and points the rifle out, aiming for a point head-level just as the trail comes into view. The man turns the corner, lugging his kill over his broad shoulders, using each hand to bundle a pair of the dead beast's legs. He stands stalk still when he sees the girl laying on the ridge. He's stunned when he sees the barrel of a gun pointed at him, but he opens his mouth to speak. "Cannibal." is all he says, softly. She hesitates but a moment before firing. The bullet passes through his pretty face.

She waits in the underbrush away from the ledge for a few minutes, making absolutely sure that nobody else will be coming to see just what they can gain from the gunshot. When she is satisfied, she goes out to the bodies with a makeshift leather sled she uses to carry large objects. A few minutes more and the beast, a boar it looks like, is loaded onto the sled. She turns her attention to the man: the back of his skull sprayed across the trail and ivy-covered brick building.

"When meat comes ambling into your home, you don't ask it its name." her mother had told her repeatedly when she was growing up. She always knew such practical things. Another ten minutes and she was heading home with bodies of both man and beast pulled along in her wake.

Mid-fall, afternoon.

The cannibal woman sits in her home, stretching the skin of her latest kill. Her home, a one-time abandoned underground shelter, is one of several she uses for sleep and storage among the overgrown buildings and forgotten land that she claims for herself. This current shelter was spared most of the destructive forces that above ground buildings suffer over time, although one wall has been sheered up with an old shell of a box-shaped machine, its square door hanging open.

Next to it, a tall rectangular chest is stood on its end, one of its doors is missing, and the other shut tight. She uses the first as a cage for live animals, though her mother used to refer to it as a "washing machine." The second object she has forgotten the name of, so she is unaware that the food she stores on its shelves is ironically its exact intended use. She sits amongst the bits of collected useful equipment; a few bottles of propane, boxes of matches, extra clothing, anything she can use to fend off the coming cold months, all of it taken from other people or found in the dilapidated buildings. There's dried and drying meats hanging from repurposed and bent coat hangers lining the walls of her dwelling.

She finishes all the stretching she's going to do today, and begins to clean her rifle. The voice of her mother echoes in her head, "Clean your weapons, every day, whether you've used them or not. Keep them from rusting. One miss-fire can get you killed, or kill you." She oils the chamber and barrel with rendered fat that she stores for that exact purpose. Finished with her work, she reassembles her rifle, and checks the door for any cracks that would let the heat and, more importantly, light out into the upcoming night. She takes some spare felt cloth that may have once been a sweater, and, kneeling down, stuffs it into the crack below the door.

There's a noise from outside her shelter – a shuffling of rock on a slippery bit of hill a few yards from the door. She freezes in position to listen to the world outside the door. There's a howl, far off in the distance, echoing from building to ruined building and overgrown, abandoned streets, but there, closer by... was that a footstep? She quietly pushes back onto her heels and leans further back into the shelter, reaching for her rifle and her precious packs of scavenged ammunition. She can hear the footsteps outside the shelter door now, rounding the building, looking for other entrances. Quickly, she loads her rifle, staying as quiet as she can.

The footsteps do a full rotation around the shelter, and pause once again in front of the door and a ways away from the shelter. She takes her rifle, and points it at the doorway, ready to shoot anyone that opens it. It's several minutes before she hears the footsteps advance. She adds slight pressure to the trigger. The footsteps reach the door. Moments pass.

There's a knock on the half rusted metal door, hesitant but strong. The sudden and unexpected noise almost causes the woman to fire her rifle, but she stays motionless, kneeling in front of the door, pointing her gun at it. This is a first for her. Nobody has ever tried to knock on her doorway before. She tries to remember what it means from stories that her mother had told her when she was a child. *Something about knocking on wood to avoid a curse, but the door is metal...* She remembers a story about what her mother called "Those damn religious people" going from home to home, knocking on doors, but why?

The knock comes again, and now it sounds impatient. *Someone is waiting out there...* she thinks. *They must want me to let them in, but they can't honestly think I'm that stupid?* She slowly moves to the door, still pointing her rifle at it, then lifts a hand to the door, and beats a pattern against it with her knuckles, jumping back as soon as she feels her flesh meet the cold steel.

For a moment, nothing happens at all. She begins to think she may have scared the person away by knocking back, when she hears the same pattern she just knocked come back from the other side of the door. Despite her fear, she finds herself amused: whoever is out there knows she is in here, and instead of leaving, they copy her.

"I'm un-armed" says a muffled male voice from the other side of the door.

"And you expect me to believe that, do you?" she manages to keep her quaking from her voice. The man says nothing. "Are you alone?" says the woman, already knowing that at least there was nobody within a few yards of the shelter.

"Yes."

"Back away from the door." The footsteps back away a few feet. "Further!" The footsteps recede further. Collecting her courage, she opens the door, feeling the cold fall wind gust in. She sees a man standing there, a few yards away. He's a few years older than she is, but dressed as shabbily, wearing collections of whatever clothing can be found, thrown together for warmth. "What do you want?" she says, after looking him over. It was true, he had no visible weapons on him.

"I saw the smoke from your fire... I just wanted to come in and rest. I've been walking for several days. Please, I just need to rest and get warm." the man says, his face radiating honesty and sincerity. He glances at the woman's rifle, still pointed squarely at his chest, and his face shows slight panic.

The woman considers firing, killing the man, and adding to her winter supplies. *But it's too close to this shelter... and he's got something about him.* The man smiles at her. "I don't suppose you have any food to spare, do you?" he says, reluctantly. She sighs, and lowers the gun to her side.

"Come in, then. But if you touch anything, you'll be dead before you know you weren't supposed to." the woman says. She stands aside to let the man through the door as he advances. He looks elated at the prospect. The man goes in and goes to the far side of the small one room shelter, sitting down on a makeshift stool. The woman closes the door behind him, sealing the cracks from the coming threat of night.

"My name is John." says the man. The woman nods at him, and sits beside the small fire, wisps of smoke beginning to fill the air before exiting through a small hole in the ceiling. John and the woman sit on opposite sides of the room in silence for several awkward minutes. "So um... what uh... what's your name?" John says, hesitantly.

The woman looks at him in the firelight. She mentally notes the shaggy hair splayed out from under a worn cap and his ill-fitting clothes. She finds amusement for a moment when she notices that his shirt was obviously once owned by a very well-endowed woman, and the lifeless withered bits of stretched cloth bare a mute witness to their past. She remembers borrowing clothing from her rather large-chested mother when she was younger, and having similar results. Minutes pass, but John doesn't seem to be worried about the lack of response. He waits, patiently, returning her stare.

Eventually she says "My name is unimportant." John grins at her.

"I see. Well, what do I call you then?" John sounds strange to the woman, like he's happy to be confusing her, enjoying some hidden joke.

"I don't care what you call me." she replies, curtly. She takes down some dried, unidentified meat and a large knife, and begins slicing it into small strips.

"Stubborn, aren't you?" he says, and laughs to himself. "Let's see... I've got to call you something. I don't suppose you'd allow something like Bernard, would you?" The woman looks up from the meat, her face a mixture of irritation and confusion. John looks at the knife in her hand. He clears his throat. "Right. Okay. How about..." he tilts his head back for a moment in thought. "Lily. That's a good name." The look of irritation faded from the newly named Lily's face, but the confusion stayed. She goes back to slicing the meat, and wonders over the meat itself – if it was sweet strips of dried human or the saltier dried pork. She honestly can't tell from looking at them in the dim light, the meats are the same off-pink color.

"What do you have to trade for your food?" she says without humor.

"Well, I did just give you a brand new name." he replies, smiling. She stares at him, still holding her knife. He gives in. "I have some ammunition."

"What size?"

".22 caliber." he says, shyly. Lily makes a sound of dismissal and rolls her eyes. "You can use the powder in them, at least." John continues. Lily thinks it over for a few moments. *I could just kill him and take the cartridges. But he's... nice.*

"Alright." she says, handing him the wooden board that she cut the meat on. "For the cartridges... and the name." she says, finally.